JASPER DASH AND THE
FLAME-PITS OF DELAWARE

A Pals in Peril Tale

JASPER DASH
AND THE
FLAME-PITS
OF DELAWARE

M. T. ANDERSON

Illustrations by **KURT CYRUS**

BEACH LANE BOOKS

NEW YORK LONDON

TORONTO SYDNEY

To the monks of Vbngoom, wherever you are

Thanks to Sam and Hannah Anderson for their expert help and advice.

BEACH LANE BOOKS
An imprint of Simon & Schuster Children's Publishing Division
1230 Avenue of the Americas, New York, New York 10020
This book is a work of fiction. Any references to historical events, real people,
or real locales are used fictitiously. Other names, characters, places, and incidents are
products of the author's imagination, and any resemblance to actual events or locales
or persons, living or dead, is entirely coincidental.
Text copyright © 2009 by M. T. Anderson
Illustrations copyright © 2009 by Kurt Cyrus
All rights reserved, including the right of reproduction in whole or in part in any form.
BEACH LANE BOOKS is a trademark of Simon & Schuster, Inc.
For information about special discounts for bulk purchases, please contact
Simon & Schuster Special Sales at 1-866-506-1949 or business@simonandschuster.com.
The Simon & Schuster Speakers Bureau can bring authors to your live event.
For more information or to book an event, contact the Simon & Schuster Speakers Bureau
at 1-866-248-3049 or visit our website at www.simonspeakers.com.
Also available in a Beach Lane Books hardcover edition.
The text for this book is set in Stempel Garamond.
Manufactured in the United States of America
0810 OFF
First Beach Lane Books paperback edition September 2010
2 4 6 8 10 9 7 5 3 1
The Library of Congress has cataloged the hardcover edition as follows:
Anderson, M. T.
Jasper Dash and the flame-pits of Delaware / M. T. Anderson ; illustrated
by Kurt Cyrus.—1st ed.
p. cm.
"A Pals in Peril Tale."
Summary: Boy Technonaut, Jasper Dash, and his friends Lily Gefelty
and Katie Mulligan travel into the mist-shrouded heart of the forbidden mountainous
realms of Delaware to try and unravel a terrible mystery.
ISBN 978-1-4169-8639-3 (hc)
[1. Adventure and adventurers—Fiction. 2. Friendship—Fiction. 3. Characters in
literature—Fiction. 4. Humorous stories. 5. Mystery and detective stories.]
I. Cyrus, Kurt, ill. II. Title.
PZ7.A54395Fl 2009
[Fic]—dc22
2008044415
ISBN 978-1-4424-0838-8 (pbk)
ISBN 978-1-4391-5608-7 (eBook)

PART ONE

AN EYE FOR AN EYE

1

When Lily Gefelty got out of bed on the morning of the big game, she looked out the window to see what kind of a day it was going to be. She discovered that it was the kind of day when a million beetles crawl out of the ground and swarm the streets, forecasting evil.

She didn't know about the evil yet, of course. She just saw the million beetles, brown and restless, dropping from trees and mobbing fire hydrants. She was not usually disgusted by beetles or anything else. But these did not seem natural.

She went to look up beetles online. Her eyes narrowed. She blew her bangs off her face. No question: It wasn't the time of year for beetles.

No, not the time of year for beetles—but as it turned out, it was indeed the time of year for evil. On that fall day, a white van had rolled into town, filled with wickedness. It had turned off  the highway at dawn. It headed for Lily's school. It was headed for the town of Pelt's big game.

Quite often, when evil comes to town, animals get restless. Horses whinny. Dogs bark at the windows. Dolphins hide their shiny pates and chitter. And in this case, the bugs, which had just settled down for the winter, crawled back out of their dens, filled with unease.

Of course, Lily didn't know that evil was in a white van, ordering sausage egg croissants at an O'Dermott's drive-thru. Neither did her friend Katie Mulligan, who knew a thing or two about evil.

When Katie and Lily were dropped off at the school gym, where the day's big match was going to take place, Katie complained, "These beetles are disgusting," kicking a few out of the way as she stepped out of her mom's car. The hard little bugs rolled a few times and skittered into a sewage drain.

"It's like a plague," said Lily, watching the beetles shiver.

"Are waterproof shoes also anti-beetle?" asked Katie, lifting her heels. "I mean, do they fend beetles off?"

"I don't know," said Lily.

"Shoes," said Katie, "should come with a complete fending list. 'These shoes fend the following.'"

Lily was thoughtful. "It's pretty late in the fall for beetles."

"Oh, lordy," said Katie. "I hope that these beetles aren't signs of a coming evil."

"Hello, chums!" called Jasper Dash, Boy Technonaut, crunching across the school lawn in Wellington boots. "What-ho and tippy tippy dingle and all."

"Eww, Jasper," said Katie, "you're crunching on june bugs."

Jasper inspected the soles of his boots. "Aha," he said. "I had noticed a jaunty crispness to my stride this morning."

"Um, Jasper," said Lily, "do you have lead weights taped to your eyelids?"

"Yes, indeed," said Jasper. With a show of great concentration, he held out his arms, puffed out his breath, and slowly raised and lowered his lids. "I want every muscle in my body to be ready for the big match today."

"Who're you playing against?" asked Lily.

"The Delaware team. From Edgar R. Burroughs High in distant Ogletown, Delaware: Delaware's state champions. They are, frankly," he said, lowering his lids and raising them again, "*frankly* supposed to be terrors. I do not mind telling you, they have left the wreckage of many another school's athletic department in their wake. Mothers weeping on the bleachers."

"Wow," said Katie. "You've really gotten into this, haven't you? I never knew you were so into sports."

"A healthy mind in a healthy body," said Jasper. "That is what I strive for." His lids opened and closed, opened and closed.

Pelt—where Jasper, Katie, and Lily lived—was not a very exciting place. It was a small town with a library, police department, some old Victorian houses covered in aluminum siding, and a street of failing stores down near the docks. To pep up business on Main Street, store owners had put mannequins out on the sidewalk, advertising dusty sweaters or pillbox hats, but the mannequins were just assaulted by gulls.

There was not much to do in Pelt. There was a museum in town, but it wasn't very exciting. Its main exhibits were on how people used to churn butter. Now, I have enjoyed my share of incredibly dull museums,* but even I found the Pelt Museum unbearable. No one really went there except third-grade field trips during their "Making of Margarine" unit. There was also an opera house in town, but it was closed and dogs lived there. At night, sighing came from the upper windows.

---

*The Joliet Insulation Museum. The Syracuse Burn-Pit. The Unsteady Walking Hall of Fame.

Given that there was not much to do in Pelt, people cared a lot about the schools' drama clubs and athletic teams. Sporting events were very well attended, and before big matches, games, and meets everyone put signs on their lawns cheering on the Pelt teams. The *Pelt Observer* always ran big stories about competitions with nearby towns.

Unfortunately, most of the Pelt athletic teams were not very good. It was a small town with a small high school and junior high, so there weren't many athletes to draw from. Their best pitcher, for example, had broken his arm playing football the previous season.

Perhaps this is why the town had become so fanatical about their competitive staring matches. Pelt's high school varsity Stare-Eyes team was well on its way to becoming state champion.

The rules were simple: Pair people off to stare at each other's faces. First person to blink or smile loses. As is said of many games: a moment to learn, a lifetime to master.

Jasper Dash, Boy Technonaut, could stare like no one else. The Pelt school system had even gone so far as to recruit him as one of their key players, even though he actually wasn't in school anymore, having received his Ph.D. in Ægyptology some years before.

Jasper was the hero of a series of largely forgotten adventure stories for boys in which he invented startling devices and rolled up his sleeves to plunge into adventure from dizzying heights. His powers of staring were almost superhuman. This is because, in the course of *Jasper Dash and the Sponge-Cake of Zama,* he had spent almost a year studying meditation and martial arts at a secret mountaintop monastery in somewhere like Nepal or Tibet. Now he stared like a force of nature. He could remain unmoving for hours. No one had ever out-stared him.

I should mention that Katie Mulligan was also the star of her own series—the Horror Hollow Series—which took place in Horror Hollow, a small, deeply haunted suburb of Pelt. Katie was brave and outspoken, especially when confronting algae that needed to be told off or blood-sucking babysitters climbing down the neighbors' walls with tots in their arms.

Lily Gefelty, the third friend in this little group, did not appear in any series of books except for this one, and for that reason she was shier than her friends. She observed things constantly and thought complicated things about what she saw. She watched through her long bangs, blowing them out of the way when there was something she wanted to inspect particularly closely. She admired her friends and wanted their series to become famous again, even though Katie's books were a few years out of date and Jasper's books were now sold mainly in large sets to J. P. Barnigan's American Family Restaurants, a mall chain that purchased books with matching bindings so they could put them up on shelves next to old-time football helmets, oars, snowshoes, cricket bats, parasols, and rustic applepeelers. This created a mood of hearty, antique good cheer. Often I have skimmed through the titles of the Jasper Dash series while eating J. P. Barnigan's deep-fried Onion Tumbleweed (appetizer) and drinking a pint of flat Cherry Coke.

Lily yearned for adventure. Though she loved her little town with her whole heart and both of her lungs, sometimes she wished that she could go to exciting places and take part in exciting events like her friends. She had never explored the basements of Inca temples like Jasper or been hunted through the bayous of Louisiana by the panting, fanged Rougarou like Katie on Labor Day weekend. Lily was a little frightened of those things—were-beasts and booby traps—but she wanted to be by the side of her two friends, leading a life less drab than Pelt's, meeting new people, seeing the world, enthusing about its strangeness and variety. Indeed, though she didn't know it, she was about to have an adventure with her friends that would take her to the far ends of the earth.

And what did our heroes look like? A good question in any age. Katie was blond and burned easily. Lily was a little stockier than Katie and wore clothes that hid most of her. Jasper looked like the outline on the GO CHILDREN SLOW sign, that is:

and in fact had been the model for that sign. It had been one of the proudest moments of his career, for he had a deep and abiding hatred of all traffic infractions and jaywalking.

It is of course the *old* GO CHILDREN SLOW sign on which he had appeared, not to be confused with:

which showed Jasper's archenemy, interdimensional criminal Bobby Spandrel, whose spherical, silver, featureless head was said to contain just one giant eyeball and whose empty cuffs shot forth photons and flames.*

The only eyeballs on display at the moment, however, were Jasper's own, as he stared with disturbing intensity at his two friends, holding open his weighted lids. "This contest against the Delaware team might well be the greatest struggle our school's athletic department has ever seen."

Lily asked, "Have your practices been going well?" She was always good at asking her friends questions when they were dying to talk.

Jasper nodded. "In the last two weeks, indeed, our ragtag band of blinkers and yawners has

---

*Faithful readers will know that Jasper defeated Bobby Spandrel's evil, pernicious plans in such novels as *Jasper Dash and the Cowpoke Caper*, *Jasper Dash in the Bladder-Jungles of Venus*, *Jasper Dash's Far-Out Hippie Adventure*, *Jasper Dash and the Hydrogen Snails of Pluto*, and *Jasper Dash and His Resounding Electric Handshake*. Whether he met Bobby Spandrel in Cairo, Egypt, or Cairo, Kentucky, Jasper always managed to smash his way into Spandrel's secret headquarters and short-circuit the villain's laser-guns before Spandrel and his evil crew blew up Fort Knox or knocked down the Eiffel Tower or kidnapped a spaceship of Martian orphans or carved Bobby Spandrel's spherical likeness into the side of Mount Rushmore beside the presidents' faces.

become a family—and a tightly knit fighting force, when need be. Coach Meyers has seen to that. He has been stern but caring."

"You mean *Doctor* Meyers?" said Katie. "The optometrist?"

"He is a fierce but fair man. He knows with almost a sixth sense when our corneas are losing their sap."

"He did a good job teaching me to put in my contacts," said Lily. "He told me that putting them in was an art, not a science."

"So, um, with the team," said Katie, "Choate Brinsley is the captain now, isn't he?"

"Yes, he is."

"What's he like? Super nice?"

Jasper shrugged, dislodging a beetle that had landed on his shoulder. "He's a sportsman and a gentleman," he said.

Lily watched Katie closely. She knew that Katie had a crush on Choate Brinsley.

Jasper mentioned, "I went to Choate's house recently for a rousing game of electronical soccer. He has a device that plays soccer on a screen."

"You went to his *house*?" exclaimed Katie. "What was it like?"

Jasper shrugged and considered. "Sound, though hard to defend from the west. To truly make it attack-proof, you'd have to have folding metallic adamantine shutters that slammed down over the glass doors in the kitchen."

"I mean, what was his *room* like? Did he have any pictures up?"

Jasper looked bewildered. "I'm not sure I understand," he said. "I really have to go. It's time to get into our uniforms."

"Okay," said Katie. "But what were the pictures in his room?"

"There was a movie poster," said Jasper. "I really must go. Beetles are crawling on my duffel bag." He shook the bag. Insects flopped onto the sidewalk. "Until later, chums?"

Lily held out her hand. "On the field of battle," she said.

Jasper smiled, grasped her hand, and shook it. "On the field of battle," he said, then saluted, turned, and jogged toward the gym doors.

"I can't believe he didn't tell me he went to Choate's house," said Katie.

"Look at the beetles," said Lily.

"I'm tired of looking at the beetles," said Katie.

"They're going away," said Lily.

Katie turned and inspected the school parking lot. It was true. Suddenly, the beetles were trundling into holes. Some dug furiously with their little pincers. Some slipped into the bark of trees. Some wedged themselves between bricks.

Other cars were pulling up by the curb and kids were getting out. They didn't seem to notice that the morning's insect plague was almost over.

Beetles whirred through the air. They landed near their nesting places. They hid. They seemed terrified.

"I wonder why they're all going away?" said Katie.

Lily hunkered down and watched a line of ladybugs flee into a storm drain.

There was a screech of tires from the street. Lily and Katie looked up. A white van had turned into the parking lot. The windows were tinted.

By the time it pulled into a spot, bucked back out, and pulled in at a better angle, there was not a beetle to be seen. The plague was over. But the danger was just beginning.

2

The doors to the gym opened, and Choate Brinsley, captain of the Pelt Varsity Stare-Eyes Team came out, dressed in a clean white shirt and khakis. He looked around and checked his watch.

"There's Choate," said Katie. "He must be waiting to meet the Delaware team and show them their locker room and stuff." She sighed. "Or he just wanted to come out and have the wind play with his hair more."

"You really should forget about him," said Lily gently.

"Omigosh. He's coming this way."

"This is the sidewalk," Lily said softly. "He has to come this way. There's grass everywhere else."

"He's still coming this way."

Katie had tried to talk to Choate several times. The first time she said hello, he looked at her like she was crazy and walked away. The second time she said hello, a few weeks later, he frowned and said, *"Huh?* Who *are* you?"* and then turned around and put books in his locker.

The night he had spoken to her like that, with such scorn and italics, Katie had actually cried at home. Lily had talked to her about it for an hour on the phone. "He doesn't know how great you are," Lily had said. Katie had wept, "And he never will!" Lily felt awful that her friend cared so much about the opinion of this one, kind of stuck-up, boy. She wished she could convince Katie to forget about him.

Now Choate stood waiting on the sidewalk, right next to Katie and Lily, looking around for his opponents. As kids walked past him toward the gym, he gave them high fives.

The van doors remained closed and locked. No one got out. There was no sign of movement behind the dark glass.

Katie slid a quick glance toward Choate, and then exclaimed loudly to Lily, "Stare-Eyes is the best sport, isn't it?"

"It's fun," said Lily. "I'm glad Jasper is making friends on the team."

Katie rolled her eyes at Lily. "I mean," said Katie, "that I really, really like Stare-Eyes."

"Oh, good," said Lily. She caught on that Choate was overhearing their conversation.

"Yup, I just love Stare-Eyes," said Katie. "I always read all the, you know, statistics and everything."

"Sure."

"I get those magazines."

"Right."

"I love it. You know who my favorite professional Stare-Eyes player is?"

"I didn't know anyone played it professionally."

Suddenly Katie realized she didn't know the names of any professional Stare-Eyes players. So she said, "Ralph . . ."—decided that was stupid, and corrected herself—"John. Ralph. I mean, Ralph . . . John . . . ston . . . ly . . . ton . . ."

Lily nodded. "Oh . . . yeah. Ralph . . . John-stonlyton." She rocked on her heels.

"Have you heard of him?"

"No," said Lily, "but then again, you know so much more about professional Stare-Eyes than I do."

Katie could tell, miserably, that Choate was still listening in, but that things weren't going too well. "Yeah," she said nervously. "Ralph, um, Johnslyunton . . . ston . . . He's the best."

"Oh," said Lily.

"I just love Stare-Eyes," said Katie. "You know how I love to stare at things."

"Oh, yeah," said Lily. "You can just stare for hours sometimes."

"Um," whispered Katie, leaning close to her friend. "Now I'm maybe starting to sound a little brain-dead. Let's go back to Ralph Johnslyuntonston."

"I don't think Choate's listening anymore,"

Lily whispered back. "And maybe next time you should make up a name that you can remember."

Katie made a sour, sassy face at Lily. Lily made a sassy, sour face back. They glared at each other. They both tried not to smile. That didn't last long. They started to laugh. Katie laughed so hard that she hit her shin on a railing and had to say, "Ow ow ow ow ow."

At that point, some of Choate's friends came along, wearing sweats, punching each other on the arm. They were yelling at each other, "Don't kill my fresh, dude! You're totally killing my fresh!"

"Choate, dude! What's going on?"

"Nothing," said Choate. "I'm just standing here waiting for the Delaware team. You think that's their van?"

"Did you see those bugs?" said one of the boys. "Dude, that was sick."

"I have this weird, bad feeling," said another boy. "In my feeling parts. Like something bad is going to happen."

Choate was still squinting into the parking lot. "That van has Delaware plates," he said. "It must be them."

The boys just had a chance to look over at the van before, with a crack, its door shot back. Eight pairs of white, boiled-onion eyes stared out from within.

It was already a cold day, but with a glimpse of those eyes, everyone standing there on the sidewalk felt an extra chill.

Slowly, one after another, the Delaware Champion Stare-Eyes Team crawled out of their van.

Their tracksuits flapped in the breeze.

3

They stood, arms crossed. The skin on their faces was tough, muscley, pearly. Their eyes looked nowhere in particular. Their mouths were confusing and lumpy, as if bristling with too many fangs. Their tracksuits identified them by number.

The driver and passenger doors opened, and a man and a woman stepped out and lined up beside their boys. The woman and the man also wore tracksuits, though instead of numbers, theirs said COACH and TEAM MOM, and were emblazoned with the symbol of Delaware—the Blue Hen State. It was a wicked-looking blue chicken with a third eye bursting through its forehead—a chicken with twelve claws, all of which clutched instruments of death: daggers, swords, deep-fry baskets, meat tenderizers, and a snickersnee.

Eight players and two coaches stood in a line. Their breath came out of their mouths in clouds.

Mechanically, they began to walk toward the gym, toward Choate and his friends and Lily and Katie.

The Pelt boys stirred uneasily. Choate looked determined, however. He clearly wanted to be a good sport. He stepped forward and held out his hand. "Hi," he said, "I'm Choate Brinsley. You must be the Delaware State Champion Stare-Eyes Team."

The line of Delawarians halted. The boy Choate had approached glared at him, mouth open. His top said #1.

"You don't have to answer him," the coach instructed #1. He looked toward some trees and said, "That guy doesn't even exist."

"He's going to fail, Daddy, isn't he?" said the boy, his eyes flickering to the coach's face. His lips were red, his mouth open, and his panting echoed in the uncomfortable silence.

"They'll all fail," said the coach.

Choate shifted from one foot to the other. He protested angrily, "I was—I was just trying to be friendly."

"There is no friendship." The coach reached into his pocket and pulled out a pack of gum. As he slid a stick out of the pack, he said to Choate, "Do you know what your insides look like?"

"No, sir," said Choate.

"Do you know what my insides look like?"

"Don," said the woman, coughing into a handkerchief, "of course he don't know your insides."

"Soon you're gonna know both," said the coach. "'Cause we're gonna yank you open and then eat you alive." He stepped closer to Choate. Choate stumbled backward. The coach said, "Stare-Eyes ain't no game for Little Timmy Timid. Stare-Eyes goes to the strong."

"We're already men, aren't we, Daddy?" said #1.

"You're all my little men. You sweat like men. You stare like men." The coach started walking for the gym doors. "Let's go."

But Katie Mulligan was in their way. She stood

in the middle of the path, fuming. "Hey!" she said. "Hey! I don't believe you people! Choate was just trying to be nice!"

"You have a friend," said the coach to Choate. "A girl friend."

Katie said, "He was trying to welcome you to our town!"

"It's a little lady. The captain of Pelt Varsity Stare-Eyes has to be protected by a little girl."

"She's a tiny thing," said #1. He smiled with ragged teeth.

At this, for some reason, all of them began to laugh. "He has a girl to protect him," said another.

"He has a *girl* to help him. A little *girl.*"

"Yeah, a *girl.*" They laughed harder.

"I'm not little!" protested Katie. She looked to Team Mom for some kind of support against the pack of boys.

The woman, however, was smiling at her own team's #1 with a mixture of adoration and cruelty. "Look at him," she said. "He's a regular monster."

"Come on," said Lily quietly, taking Katie's arm. "We should go in and get some seats."

"Another girl to protect you, kid?" said one of the boys to Choate.

The team laughed even louder. It didn't sound like real laughter, but like fake laughter for a mean show on television about poison and busting glass.

Choate looked at them angrily. Then he said to his friends, "Let's go," and they walked away toward the side door.

Abruptly the Delaware team stopped laughing. There were ten of them, all staring at Katie. She inched backward.

Lily said quietly, "Come on." She took Katie's arm again and led her off.

The Delaware team stood in a row behind them, faces expressionless, staring.

4

The gymnasium was full. Families were bustling on the risers, toddlers clomping up and down the steps. Parents sipped coffee from Thermoses, and kids from the band sold candy bars to fund more tubas. The photographer from the *Pelt Observer* wandered up and down the court, her camera swaying around her neck.

Katie and Lily made their way through the crowd. Katie exclaimed angrily, "I can't *wait* to see those stuck-up jerks from Delaware get what's coming to them during the match."

Lily knew it wasn't going to be that easy. The competition would be fierce.

Choate and his friends were talking by the door at the back of the court.

"Just a sec. I'm going to go talk to Choate," said Katie. "He must be feeling really bad."

"Are you sure you want to?" said Lily.

"I'm his fan. I should be there for him."

"He, um, wasn't so nice the last time you talked to him."

"He didn't know me. Now he sees I care."

Katie walked up to Choate and said, "I can't believe them, can you?" She jerked her thumb at the door. "They were acting like the vice-regents of the galaxy. And it's just a stupid Stare-Eyes contest."

Choate stepped toward her.

"I just can't believe them!" Katie said again.

Choate crossed his arms. He uncrossed them.

"I don't know who you are," he said, "but you"—he poked her with his finger—"stay away from me."

Katie blanched. "What?"

"I don't need a girl to protect me."

"No, wait—"

"I said I don't need a girl to protect me."

"I was trying to—"

"Go away and play with your dolls," said Choate. "And your playhouse and your dolls' Jet Ski."

One of his friends said, "She probably has a complete crush on you."

"'Oh, Choate,'" said another boy in a high-pitched voice, curling his hair around his finger, "'I'll stare into your eyes any time.'"

Katie made some sound that started with a W, mainly, but she was starting to cry, so it was hard to make out exactly. Lily went over to her and pulled her away.

"Look, she's crying," said one of Choate's friends. "The little girl's crying."

Katie turned her face away so the fluorescent light wouldn't glimmer on her tears. Lily put her arm around her friend and led her toward the stands. Lily felt sick in the pit of her stomach.

Katie wiped her eyes with her wrist. "I'm so stupid," she said. "So completely stupid."

"It's not you who's stupid," said Lily. "You just tried—"

Katie shook her head and marched forward.

The two girls climbed the bleachers. Adults were shaking hands and slapping each other on the back. A former Pelt Stare-Eyes champion back from college for the weekend was entertaining a bunch of guys with stories of the good old days: brave hearts, dry corneas, and battles to the death.

Choate and his friends were still watching the two girls. They were sniggering at Katie's tears and thinking they were very top dogs.

It was at this point that Jasper came out of the locker room, wearing a space-age uniform involving tubing and silver sparkles. He had a pinny on over it. His eyelids still sagged from the lead weights attached to them.

It was not one of his best moments.

"Hello, chums," he said to his teammates. "How do you fancy this new suit?"

Choate and his friends regarded Jasper balefully. "Jasper, dude," one choked.

"Observe," said Jasper. He pressed a button on the suit. "Ever tire, during a match, of the hours spent sitting on hard folding chairs?

This hydraulic, cushionized Stare-Eyes suit with inflatable rump is just the thing." As he was speaking, the rear of his suit grew like a muffin in the oven. "Compete in comfort. And with a built-in catheter in case you're caught short and can't scramble in time to a water closet, this—"

"What's a water closet?" asked a team member.

"Why, a W.C. A toilet," explained Jasper cheerily, his suit's rump swelling. It was huge.

"Okay, Jas," said Choate. "Okay. That's great. That's really great, but the other team might see you. Why don't you . . ." He looked carefully over his shoulder. "The other team is . . . They're real jerks, and I don't want . . ."

"It's simple as daisies to slip a pinny on over my pressurized Stare-Eyes suit! Look, chums, team pinnies! I made them for everyone."

"Get him out of here, dude," Choate muttered. "Before they see the stupid clothes."

"Jasper," said Choate's bud Giles, "come on. You need to get into some shorts."

"But this suit—"

Giles shoved Jasper back through the swinging door into the locker room.

Jasper's clanging voice came through the door. "But I want to see the other team."

The door thudded against Giles's foot. Giles held it shut fast.

"Let me out!" Jasper protested. "This is not mannerly!"

In a whisper, Giles complained to Choate, "Jasper is *so hopelessly weird*. Why does he have to be so weird? And hopeless?"

Choate Brinsley wearily rubbed his face, grimacing and stretching out his eyeholes. He scratched his head. "We are screwed," he said. "Completely. Jasper's the only one who might have a chance. And he's wearing dumb pants that . . ." Choate couldn't bear to say it. So he just repeated, "We are screwed."

A hundred feet away, Katie and Lily sat on the top bleacher. Lily inspected her friend to see how she was doing. Katie was crouched over her knees, picking with one hand at the other, trying not to look over at Choate. "Are you okay?" asked Lily.

"There's no way to make my skin hidden enough," said Katie.

Lily really didn't know what to say to this. She didn't know how to deal with Katie's romantic crises. She sat, wishing she had the instinct of the right thing to say.

"You can't worry about him," said Lily. "If he doesn't like you, then he's not good enough for you."

"I hate him and I hate myself for liking him."

"Don't hate anyone," said Lily.

Katie put her head down on her arms. For a while, it stayed there. Then she raised it. "I'm going to call my mom," Katie said. "I'm going to ask her to turn around and pick me up." She took out her cell phone. "You don't have to come with me," she said. "You should stay and see Jasper."

Lily nodded. This was an important match,

and Jasper would be hurt if none of his friends were watching him from the stands.

Katie dialed her mom.

"What's wrong, baby?"

At the sound of her mother's voice, Katie broke down and couldn't answer.

"You sound upset."

Katie wiped her face. She said, "It doesn't matter. At all. Could you come pick me up?"

"Is the game over?"

Katie said miserably, "No."

Her mother listened to the silence for a second. Then she asked gently, "It's that boy Choate, isn't it, from the Stare-Eyes team?"

Katie said it was. "Yeah, Mom. I hate him."

"Oh, honey," said Mrs. Mulligan, crooning. "Oh, baby." She sighed deeply, lovingly, across the miles. "How many times have I warned you, Kates, not to fall in love with anyone named like a prep school? I'm telling you, honey. The Choates, the Thayers, the Thatchers, the Ashtons—they'll all just break your heart."

36

Katie coughed and sniffled. "I know," she gurgled.

"Oh, honey baby," crooned Mrs. Mulligan, "little girl . . . I'm turning around. I'm turning around right now. How about I take you to the mall over in Decentville? Just you and me. A girls' day out with the two of us. We'll drive over to the mall, walk around, buy some things, and watch the terrifying emergence in the candle store of a giant ironclad worm released by seismic activity from its million years of dreamless sleep."

"Mom," said Katie, "I'm really not in the mood for a Horror Hollow encounter. I just want to go home."

"Come on, darling. People have being saying that down near the old Peterson place there's a scarecrow that walks in moonlight with a scythe, seeking a harvest of blood."

"No, Mom," said Katie. "I know you're try-ing to help, but no."

So Mrs. Mulligan headed back to the school, and Katie told Lily to enjoy the match and went out to the curb to wait for a ride home.

And it is a good thing that she left the gym, a good thing that she stood outside in the chilly autumn air—because if Katie hadn't been out there on the curb waiting for her mother, she never would have seen what she saw, and the evil that had come to Pelt might well have—

But I'm sure you're not interested in that.

5

You're interested in the big match.

Ah, the sports novel. There is nothing I love so much as a good sports novel. Never mind that my own memory of sports is limited to rope burn and dodgeball bruises. Never mind that the height of my own athletic "participation" in middle school was having my shorts pulled down in front of the girls while being forced to leap around and sing 1983's hit "Total Eclipse of the Heart."

I guess, at this point, I should give you some statistics. Isn't that how it goes in sports novels? You know, I tell you that some make-believe "Ricky" ran a 4.8-minute mile or that some imaginary junior quarterback named Chuck or Vat or Del Rosco completed 61.4 percent of his passes with five touchdowns and only two interceptions, and suddenly, like magic, you're all whipped up in the thrill of the game—you can almost *taste* the orange slices, the sweat, the blood, and the refreshing tang of Lime-Chili Blast Glacier-Ade.

So here we go. The "stats" for the Pelt Varsity Stare-Eyes team were as follows:

NAME	TIME	Br/P	VTC	LQ	#Q	Rpp	DB
Dash, Jasper	5:23:45	45.7%	10+	.03	7	18	1006.2
Brinsley, Choate (Capt.)	4:55	27.8%	7.02	3	6	29	329.7
Carnwell, Jeff	4:15	26.4%	6.9	3	6	14	347.8
Imai, Lester	4:13	26.1%	6.9	5	5	16	342.1
Barker, Zeb	3:26	23.6%	5.8	4	5	15	326.7
Jordan, Kaleem	3:17	22.8%	6.1	5	5	22	321.5
Lee, Ted	3:14	22.4%	4.2	5	4	13	318.3
Lopez, Oscar	2:58	20.3%	4.8	6	4	25	298.5
Sterling, Giles	2:49	19.7%	4.1	5	4	12	287.3
Minello, Frank	2:32	18.8%	3.9	6	4	14	276.5

Wow. I have absolutely no idea what those numbers mean, but I feel like I just ran a morning of wind sprints.

Coach Meyers, the town eye doctor, posted these stats on the locker-room wall in front of the team, except that on his copy, the letters got smaller and smaller toward the bottom of the chart.

NAME	TIME
Dash, Jasper	5:23:45
Brinsley, Choate (Capt.)	4:55
Carnwell, Jeff	4:15
Imai, Lester	4:13
Barker, Zeb	3:26
Jordan, Kaleem	3:17
Lee, Ted	3:14
Lopez, Oscar	2:58
Sterling, Giles	2:49
Minello, Frank	2:32

"Can you read the line at the bottom of the chart, Frank?" Coach Meyers barked. "Can you read it?"

"*M . . . I . . . N . . .*"

"It's *your name*, Frank! Your name is at the bottom of the list. You know who stays at the bottom? Catfish, Frank. Catfish stay at the bottom. They eat muck."

"Yes, sir."

"So I want to see some hustle out there. Got it?"

"Yes, sir."

"Good." Coach Meyers turned and slapped up another list. It stuck to the blackboard. It was the team from Delaware. "The Delaware team," he said. "Easy to beat? No. *Non. Nein. Nyet*, my friends. They are multiple-time state champions. They are fierce and hectic as tigers. Let's go over a few strategic points." With his pointer, he rapped on the list of stats.

Jasper sat, dressed now in his regular uniform, preparing mentally for the big game. He wished he were wearing his hydraulic, cushionized Stare-Eyes suit. He was astonished his team members hadn't thought it was as top-gun as he had. Still, despite their chaffing, he was determined to play his best game, to work with his fellow players, to stare, to win. He listened intently to Coach Meyers talk about each of the Delaware team's players.

"All of you will get to stare twice this match. Once in each half. You'll all have two chances— unless you all lose your first round, all eight of you, in which case there won't even be a second round." The coach knocked the board next to a name. "Delaware's Number Four, Garret Squarmus. Lester Imai, you'll be facing him in the first round. Keep cool. He does a thing with his eyebrows that makes everyone crack up. When he does it, Imai, I don't want to see you so much as purse your lips."

"Is it really funny, sir?" asked Lester. "Or is it just cheap humor?"

"Imai, *is this a laughing matter? Can you*

just tell me: Do I bust my butt with you ladies every day of the week because this is a laughing matter?"

Lester quivered and shrank. "No, sir."

"That's right, Lester. *THERE IS NO HUMOR IN THIS GAME BUT THE VITREOUS HUMOR. Got it?"*

"Yes, sir."

"Good. Now: George Wurst, Delaware's Number Two. Brinsley, you're going up against him first round. I checked his medical records: wears contacts. Use that against him." Coach Meyers tapped another name. "Jaggy Funkstein. Number Seven. Astigmatism in his left eye, and the right one can wander. Be on your guard. Don't get led astray. Are you listening, girls, or are you too busy combing your dolls' hair? Huh? Are you too busy wearing dresses and having tea parties with your pandas for a little *life-and-death thing we call Stare-Eyes?"*

There was an embarrassed silence. The concrete walls of the locker room boomed with the coach's voice. A faucet dripped in the bathroom.

Jasper wished the coach wouldn't be so harsh with the team; it was making his heart sink. He did not like one bit all the jokes about girls because girls were just not like that, and it felt like Coach Meyers was making fun of Lily and Katie and his mother and every other woman he knew. Jasper believed in winning but even more in sportsmanship. He believed that people would do their best if you just pointed out to them that they were on the side of right and goodness. He imagined sports of the future, which would be played out beneath the oceans of the world by people in finned helmets who would act as chivalrous as knights of yore.

Jasper could tell that Coach Meyers was only being mean to the team because he was scared. The Delaware team had them all frightened. The Delaware team's intimidation tactics just made Jasper more determined to win fairly, squarely, and overwhelmingly. He wanted to see Choate Brinsley and Lester Imai and all the rest of them triumph.

But the Pelt team all sat, sagging, on their benches.

Choate raised his hand, and Coach Meyers called on him. "I just met these guys," said Choate. "Just now. We're dead."

Coach Meyers swore and kicked the trash can. "Brinsley! I don't want to hear that! I kicked the trash can just now, but I was picturing you! Because right now you're sitting on us like we're a sleep-sofa! And you're eating nachos! Making yourself even heavier! Do you get it, Brinsley? You are sitting on our heads with your negativity! Do you get that solitary thought through your pretty little head?"

The team captain nodded in shame, but when the coach turned around to strike the blackboard again, Choate mouthed to his teammates, *"We're dead."*

"Okay. Number Three. Keep an eye out for—" The coach stopped. He had glanced at his watch. "There's no time, boys. No time to go on. We got to get out there." He turned to his players. "You're gonna do a great job. Right now. There is nothing between you and victory but your own fears. And airborne grit.

So I want you to head out there and kick some butt. Okay?"

There was no answering yell of "Okay" like usual. No one shouted, "Yes, sir!" and threw their eye-spritzer up into the air. They all just sat in a line on the bench, slumped left or right, their knees and shins near the floor.

But it was time.

One by one, they got up and filed out into the gym for the match of their lives.

6

Now is when the sports novel really picks up: the description of the match. This is the exciting part where I get to tell you every little detail of what happens on the court. Sit back and relax, my friends, because when we're talking about Stare-Eyes, you're in for a wild ride.

Lily leaned forward as the teams filed out onto the gym floor. There was whooping and catcalls.

Lily noticed, though, that the Pelt players already looked whipped and uneasy. They stared at the ground, and their mouths were grim. Most people in the stands didn't seem to notice. The cheerleaders made a pyramid and then, one by one, threw themselves off the top.

They hopped up and down and shouted slogans like, "That fist you felt? The punch of Pelt!" But the team didn't match their excitement.

Lily caught Jasper's eye. For a brief second, he smiled to see her sitting there watching—and then his look of utter seriousness returned.

The teams lined up on their benches. The Delaware team did not look worried or excited. Their eyes were vacant.

Oscar Lopez was the first man up, matched against Delaware's #8. The two walked out onto the mats. They sat in plastic chairs facing each other. The crowd was going wild. The ref strolled between the two and measured the distance between their foreheads with a regulation pole. Oscar closed his eyes and breathed deeply.

The ref retracted the pole, stepped back, and blew his whistle.

Like a shot, nothing happened.

The two stared intensely at each other. Delaware's #8 had slack cheeks. He breathed wetly. He did not move his hands.

Lopez licked his lips. He settled more firmly into the chair.

It wasn't long before people saw him twitching. He was trying not to blink. Something had caught in his eye. His mother screamed encouragement. She offered him pies. Lily crossed her fingers—she liked Oscar—he was in her earth science class.

But it was not his best round. His head jerked, and his eyes clenched closed, and Pelt had lost their first round to Delaware.

The next round didn't go any better. Lester Imai had a good start but ran into some trouble after forty seconds or so, due to Delaware #4's comic eyebrows—unusually bushy, ironic, and seductively friendly.

First, the left eyebrow quirked to the side—a sweet little sarcastic twitch as if to say, *"We're both friends here. It's just a game."*

Lester was prepared. Hard-faced. He didn't budge.

But then #4 began to draw his brows together. They touched, kissed, nestled like woolly worms.

It was so stupid, Lester couldn't resist laughing. And so he lost.

Round after round went this way. #7 startled Ted Lee with a grimace. Something in #5's nose made a comic, high-pitched whining noise every time he breathed, and it sent Zeb Barker into hysterical laughter. He lay clutching his gut on the mat as the crowd looked on with horror.

It was a rout.

Pelt was getting creamed by the jerkiest Stare-Eyes team in America.

7

Meanwhile, Katie stood outside in the bright sunlight. It was a little cold without her jacket. She sat down beside the steps, leaning her back against the concrete. Little brown birds gathered on the steps and fought over crumbs.

The door to the gym slammed open and shouting ricocheted out into the parking lot. Katie looked to see who was coming.

The Delaware Team Mom was smoking a cigarette and walking across the grass with a man in a brown blazer and a green necktie. They paused; Team Mom was emphasizing things with her cigarette. She said, "I'm a winner, Mr. Lecroix. I go for the gold. People bite gold to see if it's real. They bite it with their teeth. You savvy, Mr. L.?"

He nodded nervously.

"Smile more. Be a winner. Just this once." She blew smoke off to the side. "You don't know what Team Delaware risked to get these artifacts to you," she said. "Worth a pretty penny, I can tell you."

"I have the money."

"You better."

"I'll," he said nervously, "need, you know, to inspect them."

"You got it."

"I have my loupe."

"I'll bet you do, Mr. Lecroix. Step into my office." She gestured toward the van, spat nicotine on the grass, and said, "Huh. I spend so much time flexing my hands, they're like mittens of muscle. FYI."

Katie pressed herself against the side of the stairs where she squatted. Something strange was going on. She didn't know what, but she could tell that this was not your normal sports mom selling things out of the back of a van to raise money for uniforms.

She had forgotten Choate, forgotten crushes. Her Horror Hollow instincts took over, and she began to Detect.

She craned her neck around the edge of the concrete steps. The two were at the van, looking around suspiciously. Katie pulled back to conceal herself.

In a minute, she looked out again. They had opened the van's back door. They were intent on something inside. So intent that Katie could creep out and run, hunched, down the line of cars.

She could try to catch a glimpse of what was inside.

8

Meanwhile, in the gymnasium, the excitement was . . .

Oh. Pelt's still losing. Frank Minello versus Delaware #5. Noontime dazzle off the basketball backboard.

Sniffle. Sniffle. Blink. Frank Minello's eyes flapped shut. He screamed, his mouth a lima bean of agony. He threw himself forward, his face buried between his knees.

Groans. 0–5.

Really not very exciting at all.

Forget it. Let's go back outside.

9

Team Mom and Mr. Lecroix stood by the back of the van. Mr. Lecroix bent forward to see what was in the shadows. Katie couldn't see a thing. The two conspirators were in the way.

Katie craned her neck. Still she couldn't see whatever it was that lurked in the dark. Luckily Katie had hidden beside a battered Oldsmobile Delta 88 jammed diagonally in a compact-car parking space with its front tires up on the curb. The Oldsmobile Delta 88 was a car so enormously long that Katie could have slunk down its tawny side with a whole SWAT team gesturing to each other behind her and still have been masterfully concealed. She thanked the stars above for good old-fashioned gas-guzzlers with room for twenty clowns and a hurdy-gurdy and snuck forward in a crouch, her fingertips padding along the car's pockmarked surface.

When she raised her head again, she could see through the car's clouded windows, through the side windows of the van.

Team Mom was removing blankets or a tarp from something in the back.

There was a gleam.

Gold.

Something gold and jeweled and sharp was being unveiled.

Katie gasped when she saw it.

10

Inside, the crowd sat slumped on the risers. No one bothered to shout or scream. It was a massacre. The cheerleaders were no longer shouting and had given up human pyramids. They were off in the corner, playing Go Fish and mashing wads of Big League Chew into their mouths. It wasn't any use pretending that spirit or fight could win the day.

The day was basically lost to Delaware.

The score was 0–6. Choate Brinsley was up. After him, just Jasper, and then it was the end of the first half. If none of the Pelt team had won a round before then, there wouldn't be a second half. At 0–8, there was no way Pelt could win, so the game would be declared in favor of

Delaware. It would take at least one Pelt win in the first half before there was even a fighting chance of bringing home the gold, seated, bug-eyed trophy.

Combat was joined between Choate and Delaware's #2. No one moved. Pupil seized on pupil. Retinas glistened.

For a long time, there was no sound in the room except the clanging of the heaters, over which the air rippled and churned.

There is no thrill like the description of a game of Stare-Eyes.

Looking down at the players' bench, Lily considered how miserable Jasper must be, sitting there, straight-backed, waiting for his round and watching his beloved team fail again and again.

Suddenly, Choate got a look of horror on his face.

He shied away from his enemy's glance. He quivered, repelled by something—what?—that he saw—

He yelped and closed his eyes.

An angry growl rolled through the gymnasium. Two minutes and fifty-six seconds. That was all it had taken for the captain of the Pelt team to crumble. Two minutes and fifty-six seconds.

#2's eyes were mobile again, and full of ugly triumph.

Everyone was abuzz.

And Jasper was up.

11

Palms sweating, Jasper rose from the bench, dismally slapping palms with a teammate as he walked the long walk out onto the floor.

It was all too much for him. Though his team members had mocked his cushionized suit's hydraulic rump—just as they had mocked his eye-weights, his pinnies, his jetpack, and his sandwiches of nutrient fungusroast—still, they were dear to him. He was thrilled when they won a round, and they were overjoyed when he stared at an opponent unblinking for one, two, three hours. They were his team, through thick and thin, and he hated to see them lose. He knew Choate would take it hard. He looked up sadly toward the scoreboard. 0–7.

As he came forward, the town mustered some applause for Jasper Dash, their hometown hero, the Stare-Eyes champ they all could count on.

He was just about to step onto the court when Choate grabbed his arm. "Jas!" said Choate. "Something's going on!"

"I know," agreed Jasper dolefully. "The breaking of my defiant young heart."

"His eyes changed!"

"Who?"

"Number Two!"

Jasper regarded his captain carefully. "How do you mean?"

"I was sitting there—completely fine—and then his eyes changed. I mean, totally. They changed into snake eyes or cat eyes. Like he wasn't even human. You know, slitty pupils."

"I didn't see it."

"I don't think anyone else did. It's something weird. It completely freaked me out."

Jasper protested, "But surely there must be a league rule against this kind of thing. Mid-round eye substitution."

"I'm telling you, Jas, dude, it happened. It made me blink."

Jasper looked distraught. "But then that means . . . ," he said, stammering at the implication, "that means they didn't follow league regulations."

"And no one can see but us."

The referee blew his whistle.

It was Jasper's turn. It was all up to him. If he won, the game went on to a second round. If he lost, the town lost too.

He took his chair to meet his opponent.

12

Sun-blots struck from gold quivered on the walls of the van. Katie's eyes were wide with startlement.

Team Mom held some kind of sacrificial knife. It was covered in gems.

Lecroix took it from her hands and, fixing a little lens in his eye, inspected it closely. Team Mom smoked. She dawdled by the side of the van.

Lecroix nodded and handed it back to her.

She placed the knife in a wooden box and closed the lid. Now she took out some kind of idol. A dancing woman with a lute in her hands and a coral carnation blooming where a head should be. Lecroix squatted and peered at the statue.

Meanwhile, Team Mom uncovered another treasure. A boxy something . . .

Katie swiveled from side to side, trying to see through the row of windows. She ducked and slithered back along the side of the Delta 88.

She popped her head up near the trunk. Team Mom had taken out the artifact and held it in her arms for Lecroix's inspection.

It was a model of a building. On each of its many square towers there were little antennae.

Mr. Lecroix looked it over. He seemed very excited. He nodded again and again, and once kissed his fingertips. He rubbed his hands on his pants.

Katie shifted to try to see more clearly. Mr. Lecroix was obviously thrilled. The artifact looked like it was made out of cardboard. The antennae were plastic spoons.

Mr. Lecroix smiled. Team Mom slid the model back into the van. While she draped a tarp over the objects, Lecroix got out his wallet.

He was counting money. A lot of money.

Katie held her breath. She didn't know what was going on, but she could tell it was not legal.

Lecroix held a stack of bills out for Team Mom to take. She licked her finger and reached for the money. Her hand—

"Hey! Katie!" yelled Mrs. Mulligan. "Yoo-hoo, honey! What are you doing crouched over like that?"

Katie jolted with surprise. So did Lecroix and Team Mom.

Katie's mother called, "Straighten your back, darling! You're beautiful! Is crouched over next to a Delta Eighty-eight the kind of posture they teach at this school?"

Team Mom's eyes were trained on Katie Mulligan. They were suddenly very thin and evil.

Katie tried not to meet the woman's gaze.

Katie's mother pushed the passenger-side door open. "Hop on in, honey!" she said. "If you're done giving yourself scoliosis."

Katie slid into her mother's car.

"Are you okay?" asked Mrs. Mulligan.

"Yeah, but I just—"

"Your girl was spying," said Team Mom, her face huge in the window.

"No I wasn't," said Katie.

"I'm sure she was," said Katie's mom, scraggling Katie's hair with her hand. "You might not recognize her, but my daughter solves mysteries and fights evil? Famously?"

"Mom, you really don't have to—"

"Toot your horn? Are you kidding? I am so proud of you. You are my little angel." Katie's mother explained to Team Mom, "My daughter is named Katie Mulligan. Katie Mulligan? Maybe you recognize her from her series of books, Horror Hollow?"

"Katie Mulligan," said Team Mom. "Hm."

"Ring a bell?" said Mrs. Mulligan. With a cheerful little laugh, "Well, she'll be ringing plenty of bells soon enough if she stays hunched over like that."

Nobody laughed. Katie was confused. "It was

a joke," said Katie's mom. "About the Hunch-back of Notre Dame. He had a hunched back. And he rang bells. He was a bell ringer."

"A bell ringer," said Team Mom.

"Ding, dong," said Katie's mother. "Don't I know you from the PTA?"

"No," said Team Mom, "I am from Delaware."

"Oh, Delaware," said Katie's mother politely. "Huh. Delaware! That's nice. Aren't there a lot of . . . Don't you have . . ." Katie's mother tapped the steering wheel with her thumbs. "Wow, Delaware. Well, welcome! Nice to meet you!"

Team Mom blew a stream of smoke into the Mulligan's car. "I'm sure," said Team Mom to Katie, "that we will meet again."

And with that, she walked away across the parking lot.

13

In the auditorium, things did not look good. Lily could barely stand to watch. Jasper was haggard, gray, his eyes red, his mouth open, his whole body sagging forward and swaying. Meanwhile, his opponent, #1, sat enthroned in his folding chair and radiated triumph.

To Jasper, every second was agony.

The round had started out well enough. Jasper, confronted by his enemy's eyes, sank into the meditative half sleep he had learned at the secret mountaintop monastery during days wreathed in fog, paired off with a wrinkled gingko tree. The world faded like an illusion too dull to sustain. Jasper could distantly hear sounds, as if through water—the dropping of a pen, the thumping of the radiators—but everything seemed so far away that nothing, he felt, could touch him.

But it was at that point that the eyes—the animal eyes in the human face—bit into his vision like fangs. Illegal mid-round eye substitution.

Jasper faltered—snapped out of his trance—and saw #1, serpent-eyed, staring at him.

He had maintained his control. But he could feel himself being mesmerized by that monster gaze, as he had once seen the giant cobras of Uttar Pradesh, swaying side to side, hypnotize their mammal prey—a brush-whiskered English High Commissioner of Trade—before striking.

Jasper could not hold on much longer. His eyes were dry. The room flashed negative and positive. He struggled to re-achieve the trance that would allow him to sit out the round in serenity, withdrawn from the world.

But the serpent eyes glared at him, demanding that he yield.

He would not. He tried to straighten his back. He tried to steel himself for another minute. *Just . . .* , he thought, *one minute . . . If I can make it one more minute . . . and then one minute after that . . . and then one minute after that . . .*

Jasper had never met anyone who could beat him at Stare-Eyes.

Trembling, he gawked athletically. Seconds went by.

It had been a half an hour. Everyone had fallen silent. People sat nervously in the stands. They folded and unfolded programs. Two girls cried into Dixie cups.

No, things did not look good for Jasper and Pelt, there in the gym.

And then, in the silence, Choate Brinsley put his hands together. People looked at him, startled.

He began to chant: "J-Dash! J-Dash! J-Dash! J-Dash!"

It was stupid, but someone took it up; and then someone else; and then a third. And soon the whole crowd had joined in, clapping together, calling out Jasper's name.

And because of them, Jasper remembered his town. He remembered community. He remembered that everyone was there not just to see him staring, but to be together, because people need to be with other people and dogs and elms—and Jasper felt the whole enthusiasm of the town of Pelt behind him, the hopes of the village mailman and butcher and tinker and the little toilet-paper peddler who wobbled up and down the streets on his sparkly bike, piping, "TP! TP! TP for sale!"

And so Jasper, borne up on the wave of chanting, sat up again. He focused his gaze once again on the serpent eyes, the bleached face, the flat mouth before him. He surfed on the beat of the chant. He let it take him. He let things fade.

He was going back into his trance. Once there, nothing would be able to dislodge him.

The slitted eyes faded. Jasper floated free, in space. Time passed. All physical things were only shadows. Life was but a dream.

Until suddenly, a scream knocked him—not a scream heard, but a scream felt.

Someone—somewhere—was calling his name. Not a crowd. Someone miles away. Someone whose very life was in danger.

Jasper! Jasper Dash!

Someone needed him.

HELP! JASPER DASH, I NEED YOUR HELP! the voice rang out within him.

Thinking—*But who?*—Jasper blinked and looked around.

He seemed to be in a room with people shouting and booing and hissing. He couldn't remember who they were or imagine why they seemed angry, or why the fellow sitting across from him might look so smug.

Someone, somewhere, needed Jasper Dash. He rose and gave a mighty cry.

Then he remembered he was in the gymnasium of Pelt High.

And he had just blinked. And he had just lost the game to Delaware.

14

Jasper Dash's house was the only one on the street with a hangar and a missile silo. The other houses were ranch style, meaning flat. They had basketball hoops in their driveways and drum kits in their two-car garages. Jasper's house had walls of block glass and panels of metal, curved stucco corners, and huge, white, saucer-shaped decks, below which wild hedges grew.

After the game, Lily went to Jasper's house for lunch to console him. Katie rode her bike over to meet them there. She no longer was thinking about Choate's meanness. She was thinking about stolen artifacts.

Lunch wasn't ready, so Mrs. Dash sent them out to walk in the woods until the macaroni was cooked. It would take a while to cook. The Dashes had a microwave, but it didn't work very well. Jasper had invented it himself years before. It was so old and primitive that when it was on, you could actually see the atoms bouncing around inside like the numbered Ping-Pong balls in the state lottery.

Having set the table, the three put on their coats and set out behind the house along the broad, leafy trails where Jasper had, a lifetime ago, zipped along on his first vehicle, the Astonishing Gasoline Velocipede. They walked past hillock and swamp.

It was autumn. The leaves were brown or off.

The three of them walked along in a line. Their breath came out in steam. "Don't worry, Jasper," said Katie. "There's nothing you could have done."

"I let my team down," said Jasper. "I wanted to show them that I could be one of them, though I may dress differently. Inflatably. And instead, why, Katie, I lost the game for them."

"First of all, you didn't lose the game for them," said Katie. "Everyone lost their own round. And second of all, I have to say, I don't think Choate Brinsley is so great, anyway. It's okay to let him down."

Lily kicked up leaves with her toe and said, "Jasper, it sounds like the Delaware team cheated somehow."

"Illegal mid-round eye substitution," said Jasper, shaking his head. "Completely unnerving. This league has gone to the dogs."

Lily asked, "What do you mean when you say Number One's eyes were different?"

"Like a cat's eyes. You know what a cat's eyes look like?"

"No," said Katie. "Because my cat is so completely lazy. I've never seen her eyes actually open."

"Which?" said Lily. "Trish?"

"She didn't move for a week. Dad thought she was dead. We were about to bury her when someone noticed the chicken was missing from the counter."

"Maybe," interrupted Jasper firmly, "his eyes were more like a snake's."

"That's the only pet lazier than a cat," said Katie. "They move once a month."

"You don't think it was your vision playing tricks on you?" said Lily.

"I am afraid not," said Jasper. "Choate saw it too."

"Choate," muttered Katie, more to herself than to anyone else.

"Katie, you said that you saw something, too?" asked Lily.

"Hold, chums," said Jasper, putting up his hand. "There's one more detail. When I was in my trance, someone called out to me. Through ESP. Someone, somewhere, needs help."

"Who?" asked Lily.

"That I don't know," said Jasper. "I just

know that they somehow reached me on the astral plane."

"You should just get a cell phone," said Katie. "Or inventorate one."

"There is something sinister going on," Jasper mused.

"Yeah," said Katie. "I've got to tell you about the van."

They turned a corner onto a broad, rutted track softened by moss and fallen pine needles. They walked down an avenue of ancient concrete bunkers built into the hillside, covered with grass and spruce trees and birches. The doors were massive and rusted shut. They had not been opened for many years.* Katie narrated the story

---

*The bunkers on Jasper's property were experimental bunkers. Some of them were his, and some of them were leftover alien experimental bunkers from olden times. There were lots of ancient tunnels that ran under the ground there, too, and old control rooms, and I think some things lived down there, maybe. There were probably routes to places like the Diamond Realm and the Court of the Fungus Lords. But that's not what this book's about. It's about Stare-Eyes. Okay? All right? If you're so bloody interested in the bunkers, why don't you go write a story about them yourself?

Your guess is as good as mine.

of her going out to sit on the gymnasium steps and what she had seen there: the mysterious deal between Mr. Lecroix and Team Mom.

"Mr. Lecroix," said Jasper. "I know that name."

"But here's the weirdest treasure in the van," said Katie. "A model of some kind. It was of a building, like a fortress or something. Everything else she showed him was made out of gold and silver and coral. This was made out of cardboard."

Jasper stopped in his tracks. "And it had spoons on the roof."

"Yeah!" said Katie. "Plastic spoons! And you knew, how?"

Jasper gazed into the spruce. He said nothing.

He turned around and started marching back to the house.

"What's going on?" Lily called to him, running after.

"This is big. This is very big." Jasper frowned.

"And I remember now who Lecroix is. Everything falls into place."

"Who is he?" asked Katie.

"Ernest Lecroix is the director of the Pelt Museum. I once went there to donate artifacts from Venus and ancient Greece."

"I didn't know there were things from you in the Pelt Museum," said Katie. "That's cool."

"There are *not* things from me," said Jasper. "Why, Mr. Lecroix did not believe that I had been to Venus or to ancient Greece. He rejected my donations, using as an excuse that he wished to stand by the museum's proud concentration on traditional butter-churning techniques."

"How did you know about the spoons?" said Lily. "What's going on, Jasper?"

"What does all this mean?" asked Katie.

Jasper stopped in his tracks and turned to them. "It means, my friends, gather up your khakis and pith helmets. We are going, chums, to Delaware."

"And I remember now who Lucrettia Treva
tting rain into place."

"Where her," asked Katie.

"Baron Laciron was the director of the Pak
Museum. I once went there to donate artifacts
from Vesna and ancient Greece."

"If I don't know these were they," Sam would

15

"I've been to Delaware," said Katie. "My uncle Brad worked there as a door-to-door knife salesman."

Lily was lost. She didn't see how any of this added up.

Jasper, however, was adamant. "We'll take the Gyroscopic Sky Suite,"* he said.

He was anxious and moody. He wouldn't look at Katie or Lily. He stared into the sumac and the tangled, gray grass.

Then he sighed and began speaking. "For

*The Gyroscopic Sky Suite was Jasper's invention: a flying set of rooms that clamped on to the side of luxury hotels. It first appeared in *The Clue of the Linoleum Lederhosen*. If you haven't read that book yet, this might be a good time to kick off the covers, jump in your go-cart, and roll downhill to the nearest bookstore to purchase seven.

almost a year, I studied the ancient arts of meditation at a secret monastery in the mountains," he said.

"We know," said Katie. "It's in *Jasper Dash and His Vertiginous Propeller Suit.*"

Lily corrected softly, "I think it's *Jasper Dash and the Sponge-Cake of Zama.*" And to Jasper she said, "You went to Tibet."

Jasper's mouth was thin. "It was not," he admitted, "precisely Tibet." He sighed, and the autumn wind blew a lock of his fair hair across his forehead. "It was, in fact, in the ancient, eldritch mountains of Delaware."

Katie and Lily exchanged a Look.

"The mountains," said Katie. "Of Delaware."

Jasper, gazing off into the dark and knitted hemlocks around them, whispered, "The path was long, through the jungle. That way was not easy going, chums. Once I left the borders of Maryland, every moment was a struggle. Wounded by a panther, hunted by diamond smugglers, knotted up with cobras, with no hope of finding the lost temple I sought, I passed out unconscious in my hiding place in the roots of a baobab tree.

"I awoke to find myself swaying in a stretcher, being carried through a courtyard at the top of the world. I was in the monastery of Vbngoom, the Platter of Heaven. The monks who carried me were strong as oxen, yet gentle as—"

"Jasper," said Katie, "there are no mountains in Delaware."

"Their heads were shaved, and they wore robes of forest green. Some wore helmets or they—"

"Water slides," Katie said. "There are water slides in Delaware. Putt-putt golf. Shoe outlets. Stores that sell drums and electric guitars. But no mountains."

"For almost a year, I remained there hidden in the fastness of Vbngoom, wandering its court-yards and cloisters. I studied and spent hours in silence, staring into the eyes of the monastery tiger. I spent whole days smelling a single jasmine flower. I laughed; I did not speak. With another novice, soon my friend, Drgnan Pghlik, I learned the ways of martial arts and stillness."

"You learned the ways of nutcase," said Katie. "Are you sure you didn't spend an hour facedown in your custard? And have to be revived in a clean, white place?"

"Jasper," said Lily, "what does this have to do with the Stare-Eyes team cheating?"

"Because the cardboard model Katie saw—the building with the plastic spoons on the turrets—that is a sacred object. That is the only known model of the lost monastery of Vbngoom."

16

Jasper explained more details of the situation to them over macaroni and cheese. The food was nice and hot after the chilly outdoors. Mrs. Dash, her hair a perfect bell, sat on a stool, reading a gardening magazine.

Jasper could barely chew, in his excitement. He said, "All of the objects you saw in the back of the van, Katie—they were all prized by the monks. They should be sitting in the temple at Vbngoom. They must have been stolen." Jasper tapped his fork on his plate. "I believe I have deduced what is going on."

Lily and Katie paid close attention.

"The Delaware Stare-Eyes team," said Jasper, "is just a ruse. A front. They are actually smugglers—

art thieves. There is at the moment a big market for sacred artifacts smuggled out of countries and sold to museums. This, indeed, is the Stare-Eyes team's real game. Somehow, they have stolen these sacred objects from Vbngoom. Then, disguised as an athletic team, they sneak the stolen antiquities across the border from Delaware. They sell them illegally to museums like Pelt's."

"How do you know?" asked Lily.

"Several reasons. The theory fits with the conversation Katie overheard. Second, the monks of Vbngoom would never allow those treasures to leave their walls. Somebody must be there plundering their monastery. Third, I believe that the so-called Delaware Stare-Eyes champions win their dastardly victories by tapping into the ancient power of the monastery. And, fourth, last, and finally, I believe that the person calling me for help when I was entranced was none other than my long-lost friend, Brother Drgnan Pghlik."

"Honey," said Mrs. Dash from across the

kitchen, "you're not going back to Delaware, are you?"

"Could you tell him," said Katie, "that there are no mountains?"

Jasper rose. "Mother," he said. "I must return. I must again cross the bleak and blasted border of New Jersey. There is no other way. It shall not be for long this time." He went and embraced her.

Katie and Lily put down their forks. Mrs. Dash was always lonely. Desperately lonely. She had lived for years in this crumbling house of the future and had raised Jasper completely by herself, Jasper's father being a beam of highly concentrated information emitted from the region of the Horsehead Nebula.

Jasper and his mother held on to each other. "Oh, Jas. Jas," she said, and she started to cry, cradling the back of his head. "Last time, you were gone for so long."

"My friend is in need," said Jasper.

She closed her eyes, kissed the top of his head, and whispered, resigned, "Someone always is."

"Will you be okay?" he asked.

She nodded. "I always am. I have my committee meetings. Tomorrow is the benefit dinner for the Save the Chameleon Fund. The Decentville Zoo thinks their chameleons are either dead, missing, or plaid."

"We won't be long," said Jasper. "Just a few days. We'll take the Gyroscopic Sky Suite."

"And your woolen socks," said Mrs. Dash. "It gets cold up in those mountains."

At the word *mountains*, Katie picked up her fork and threw it down again.

And so, our heroes were off to Delaware.

Now they are at their homes, packing. Lights from passing cars slide across their bedroom walls. They have their suitcases open and are zipping up their sponge-bags. Lily and Katie are slightly at a loss as to what clothes to bring.

But before I move the scene of this gripping tale to the Blue Hen State, I need to make a couple of things clear.

Occasionally, an author will go away on a vacation for a week somewhere—someplace where the food is spicy and he doesn't recognize all the fruit—and he'll have a really great time, and the culture will seem very exotic, and once he gets home to Ohio, or Minnesota, or Maine, he'll decide to write a novel about it all. He'll base the book on his one meager week staying at a Hilton Hotel a mile outside of the city he's describing and his reading of a few library books with names like *The Jewel in the Dagger*, or *Siberian Uplift*, or *A Cornish Country Autumn*, or Time/Life's *The Glory of Slurbostan*.

And so, instead of the book being written by someone who has lived there by the side of the ruins described and has spent their life eating those little crunchy fried things, you get a book by someone who really only has a cartoon idea of what a place is like, a bungled pantomime of information about customs and foods and wacky clothes and music. There are many books of that kind, written by people who have barely traveled to the destination they write about. You can't trust them.

For this reason, to put you at ease, let me reassure you: This is not one of those books. I didn't write this novel with a week's research and a couple of foldout brochures. I wouldn't do that to you. No, my friends, I solemnly promise: I have never once been to Delaware in my life. I can state with confidence that I am completely ignorant. I am a moron. I know absolutely nothing about the place. Everything I say is simply an uneducated guess.* You are not in good hands. You are in incredibly clumsy, incompetent hands.

Of course, it is important to us here at Simon and Schuster that everything in our books be entirely accurate. I would hate it, for example, if you were actually from the state of Delaware and you found some inaccuracy in my portrayal.

So, for that reason, if you do discover there is some difference between this book's portrait of the state and the reality, please write a note describing the problem in full. Send it, with a

---

*Wait—wait! Now I am remembering that I did indeed pass through Delaware for about twenty minutes on the way from New Jersey to Maryland. All I remember was the tolls on the interstate were really high, given I was there for less than a half an hour. I think they were about $4.50.

self-addressed, stamped envelope, to:

The Governor of Delaware
Office of the Governor
Tatnall Building
William Penn Street, 2nd Floor
Dover, DE 19901

I'm sure they'll get back to you.

In the meantime, I hear the whirr of engines. Jasper Dash, Lily Gefelty, and Katie Mulligan have set off in their Gyroscopic Sky Suite. They are flying over highway, suburb, and mall.

They are headed for the jungles and mountains, the beaches and subaquatic cities, the volcanoes and ziggurats, the deserts, caverns, lost temples, and spires . . . of Delaware.

PART TWO

DARKNESS IN DOVER

17

That morning, if the inhabitants of New Jersey had looked up from their shoe-shines, they might have seen, in the sky above them, a strange, shingled rocket supported from the bottom of a jet with a large silver girdle. This was Jasper Dash's remarkable Gyroscopic Sky Suite. It was well on its way to Delaware.

Inside, in the expertly riveted control room, our three heroes were lost in their own thoughts. They gazed in different directions: at the oxygen tanks, or the dials, or the pedals.

Jasper was full of worry for his friends at the monastery of Vbngoom, the gentle monks, but he was also glad to be going back to a place he loved, where he knew what was what and people didn't rag him cruelly for having come up with a dandy new invention.

Lily was excited, though the only way she showed it was by jamming her fingers into the heels of her sneakers and wriggling them as she sat, hunched over, on a swivel chair. She didn't know what to expect, but she was very glad to be along for the ride.

Katie, on the other hand, was mainly irritated. She was sick of boys' pride, the way boys could be so conceited. Especially certain athletic boys named like prep schools. And she was angry that she— who had outwitted giant brains and outrun giant centipedes—actually cared what a boy thought. She was mad at herself, and bunched up her lips in frustration.

Lights on the control panel flashed softly. Jasper checked a map and called instructions into the command snorkel.

Lily asked him, "Are we headed for the monastery in the mountains right now?"

"Mountains," muttered Katie.

"No, Lily," Jasper answered. "The location of

the monastery is so secret that even I do not know where it lies. Vbngoom, the Platter of Heaven, is shrouded in mystery. We will have to land in Dover, often called the capital of Delaware, and find a guide. From there, we will head into the jungle. We will attempt to retrace my steps from the last time I found the monastery."

"Jungle," muttered Katie. She pinched a toggle switch hard between her fingers, just to have something to pinch.

"I worry, however," mused Jasper. "There is an ancient myth that Vbngoom moves at times of trouble from mountain to mountain. Who knows where it lies now? Who knows how we shall find it?"

Jasper peered into the Oculo-Scope and made some adjustments to cranks and dials. He said solemnly, "We are passing into Delaware." He reached over and opened the iron shutters so the girls could see out of the portholes.

They were in the shadows of the mountains. The clouds strayed between the white peaks, and the airborne Sky Suite itself was no higher than those icy bluffs and frigid cliffs. Down below, deep in the valleys, lay forests and rivers, the haunt of panther and serpent. Lily caught sight of ruined aqueducts and vine-covered towers, ziggurat steps moldering in the lush undergrowth.

"New Castle County," Jasper said. He sighed and laid his head against the metal wall. "We face great challenges, fellows, and great danger. Below us lies a realm of wonders and terrors, a land that time forgot, or chose specifically not to remember." He gestured out the window to the peaks and crags. "For one hundred years, Delaware has been cut off from the other states, isolated completely as a result of its overpriced and prohibitive interstate highway tolls. For one hundred years, almost no one has gone in or come out. Only the bravest of explorers have penetrated this exotic land. We must take care not to attract the attention of the cruel tyrant who rules this state—"

Katie had been wrapping an oxygen tube around her wrist in sheer irritation for the last several minutes and now could stand to listen no longer. "You mean the *governor*?" she demanded. "The governor of Delaware?"

Jasper said quietly, "No, Katie. Much worse than that. Thirty-two years ago, the governor of Delaware was chased out by a crazed military dictator, who now rules from Dover with an iron fist—a man known only as His Terrifying Majesty, the Awful and Adorable Autarch of Dagsboro."

Jasper peered again into the Oculo-Scope and made some adjustments on the control panel. He said, "Recently, a few tourists have been allowed in under strict government supervision. But we don't want the tyrant's eyes upon us. He would love to get his hands on the monastery of Vbngoom, and we must make sure that he can't follow us there. If he were to find the monastery, he could force the monks to show him how they gained their sacred psychic powers. Why, then he could be even more cruel and tyrannical than he is now.

"I hope that by attaching the Sky Suite disguised to one of the hotels in the capital, we might evade the notice of the Autarch and his goons. That way we can explore the jungle without the Ministry of Silence interfering."

"The Ministry of Silence?!" said Lily.

"That is the name the Adorable Autarch of Dagsboro has given his spies. Beware of them. They are everywhere in the capital. Closets. Secret rooms. The tap water."

"Okay," said Katie, "I really am only going to say this one time. There is a governor of Delaware, there is no such thing as the Ministry of Silence, there is no way spies could be in the tap water, and there are no—hear me—no no no mountains in—"

"Behold: Dover. Capital of Delaware," said Jasper.

Its domes and minarets lay before them, glowing gold in the sunlight amid the hanging gardens, the pleasant palaces, the spired roofs of ancient temples; in the harbor, the purple-sailed ships of Wilmington plied the waves, and the dragon-headed prows of the barbarian kingdoms to the south dipped their oars in wrinkled waters while plesiosaurs turned capers at their sides. The Zeppelin-Lords of frosty Elsmere drifted above the city, their balloons gilded with the tropical sun, eating sherbet on their porphyry verandas. Huge tortoises fifteen feet across lumbered through the widest avenues, carrying nomads' tents upon their backs. Processions wandering through the streets glittered with gold and ancient costumery. But everything was not beautiful: Katie and Lily saw also the huge cement housing blocks looking burnt and desolate, where the hapless citizens lived in fear of their ruler. They saw the brown rivers, the broken factories, the Autarch's armies drilling on a baseball field.

They saw the lovely and the awful, the jeweled and the broken, the noble and the sad. In short, they saw Dover.

"I think," said Lily, "we better let Jasper just tell us what's what."

Katie nodded with her mouth wide open. "Yeah . . . ," she said slowly. "Yeaaaaaaah."

Jasper was all business. "Now, fellows, time to attach the Sky Suite to the side of a hotel.

We've got to be careful. If we attract attention, it will make our trip to Vbngoom all the harder. There will be government agents everywhere."

He spoke into the snorkel to the robot in the jet above them, calling out numbers and directions. "Adjust thirty-four point nine! Modulate to the plane of the ecliptic point oh oh seven! Prepare to disengage zirconium girdle!" He turned to the girls. "Hold on to your seats, chaps. You may recall that there is a little bump when the Sky Suite—"

"Oh no," said Katie. "I remember."

"Oh, gosh," said Lily.

"Oh, wowzers," said Katie. There was a click. "Oh, help. Oh, help. Oh—" But Katie didn't finish her sentence. Because they suddenly were falling and screaming—and their bellies were flipping around like trout in a washer—and they saw a cheap cement government hotel spiraling toward them—streaked with soot—and then—

BAM!

. . . which took up a whole page.

They opened their eyes. Katie coughed. Lily blew the hair out of her eyes. Jasper smiled. "Jupiter's moons," he said, "we've done it. We're attached. We've clamped on to the wall. We are now rooms twenty-three A through E of the Dupontville Fine Excellent View Stay Hotel, Dover. We have landed in utmost secrecy."

There was a cracking. There was a popping.

With a scream, with a crash, with a horrible bump, they fell again.

The Dupontville Fine Excellent View Stay Hotel had not been built very well. The Gyroscopic Sky Suite had just pulled down the whole wall of the place on top of it.

18

But let us go back a day and see what happened elsewhere while all the excitement was going on in the gym in Pelt. If, the day before, we had been in Vbngoom Monastery, the Platter of Heaven, this is what we would have seen: a boy walking down a dark stone hallway, carrying a vat of lentil soup to gangsters.

His head was shaved, like the heads of all the monks of Vbngoom. He wore robes of green. His bare feet shuffled on the flagstones. On his face was a look of determination.

His name was Drgnan Pghlik.

He passed down a flight of steps so old that the first men to use them had walked on all fours. The walls were painted with gods and oxen.

The boy shifted the huge tin vat in his arms and bowed through a low doorway.

Drgnan Pghlik had lived in the monastery of Vbngoom for almost the whole of his life. He had grown up in Vbngoom. He loved it there. He knew all the cloisters and the towers, the covered paths and secret gardens, the highest pinnacles of rock and the chambers deepest underground. He had taken his vows of obedience and kindness. He had promised never to tell a lie. He had spent months without speaking a word. In return, he was taught by the old, wise monks. They told him to speak in riddles, which he loved.* He studied inscriptions carved in stone and learned the art of monastic combat so that one day he could become one of the order's Protectors and go forth into the land to fight evil and ignorance.

---

*All monks speak in riddles. Whenever one of King Arthur's knights, for example, meets a monk in the Forest Perilous, all the monks say are things like "Pride, my son, is like four white pigs in a clearing." Then they tell a story that isn't an explanation of anything except pigs. They never say useful things like "You know, you can get the bloodstains out of that coat with some salt and seltzer," or "Dude. Giant behind you."

But now, his mountain home was threatened. A few weeks earlier, gangsters from Dover's mean streets had busted down the monastery gates and started swinging their guns around, demanding to be shown the treasure rooms. They lit cigars in the sacred flames. Chambers that had lain silent for centuries now echoed with calls of "Hey, youse guys!" and "Wouldja feast your ever-lovin' peepers on this!" The gangsters seized the old, holy treasures. They made fun of the old, holy monks. And they did not leave. They took control of Vbngoom. Since then, everyone in the monastery had lived in fear.

The worst of all of them were the gangsters' kids. Eight boys had come with the mob. They were awful. They made fun of the littlest monks, who were only nine or ten years old. The gangsters' kids kicked the monks and shined their shaved heads like bowling balls. They tortured the young novices with all sorts of mean little injuries: with Noogies and Monkey Bites, with Twister-Burns and Swirlies, with Seal Slaps,

Nettle Wipes, and Goody McCoy's Grouchy Stump. There was no end to the indignities. Thank goodness they were gone at the moment, posing as a Stare-Eyes team so they could take stolen artifacts out of the state without the government noticing. Things had been quieter around the monastery since they left. It seemed, many monks whispered, like it might be an opportunity.

As Drgnan walked down the corridor, the tub of soup weighing heavily in his arms, he passed courtyards where monks now labored for the mob. Their robes were smudged with dirt. Many of them worked building a road up to the monastery so the gangsters could come and go more easily. As Drgnan walked by them now, they stumbled along in rows, brown with dust, bowed over beneath heavy sacks of rocks.

Not for much longer, he thought. He ducked behind some pillars. He put down the vat. The soup inside swayed from side to side.

Drgnan Pghlik looked both ways. In a split second, he had reached into his robe and pulled out a small bottle of pink liquid. He popped out the lid with his thumb, dumped the whole bottle into the lentil soup, and shoved the vial back into his pocket.

Sleeping potion. Given to him by Brother Herbalist, who had concocted it out of mysterious liquors, rare flowers, and a lot of cough syrup.

Drgnan Pghlik had just put enough sleeping potion in the soup to knock out the whole mob. Once they ate it, they'd drop flat and start snoring—too dizzy to shoot off their pistols. Once the mobsters had fallen asleep, the monks would rise up and truss them.

Never again would these bad men steal sacred treasures. Never again would they yell from tower to tower in their brassy lingo: "Hey, Checkers! Be a sweet pea and stand guard, wouldja? I gots to whizz like all outdoors." (Echo in the mountains: *whizz like all outdoors . . . whizz like all*

outdoors . . . like all outdoors . . . all outdoors . . .)
Once again, the bridges and chambers would be filled only with talk of kindness and the whispering of ancient riddles.

The boy stilled any sign of sly excitement on his face. He showed no expression whatsoever. He picked up the vat of soup and carried it down the corridor that led to the monastery's refectory.

In the years before the mob had come, the monks had all dined here together, happily discussing the news of the day while eating one long root laid down the length of the table. Now, this was where the mobsters hunched over their entrées, demanding steak.

Drgnan gently knocked the tin tub against the door. A mobster opened it a crack and stuck the muzzle of his gun through. "Who's there?" asked the mobster.

"It is young Brother Drgnan Pghlik. I have come with the lunch from the kitchen."

"What's lunch, kid?"

"Lentil soup."

"Yoinks." The mobster turned away and announced to the room, "Kid in a dress with the feed."

"Let the squirt in," said one of the bosses.

The door opened. Drgnan Pghlik entered with his poisoned meal.

The dining room of Vbngoom was simple, made of mud, stone, and plaster, painted white and a dark clay red. High windows looked out across the mountain peaks. At the old wooden tables sat the gangsters in front of their bowls. They growled and muttered to one another.

Drgnan Pghlik had been taught to be peaceful and serene. He did not feel serene or peaceful now—now that he had a huge pot of poisoned stew he had to feed to twenty toughs.

Almost all of the gang's leaders were there in the dining room. The top boss never appeared. Drgnan Pghlik had no idea even what he looked like. He knew all too well, however, the sour faces of the mob's other big shots. They stood around the tables eating carrots and exchanging business cards.

"Serve it up," said one of the bosses.

Drgnan Pghlik reached into the pot, picked up the ladle, and began to spoon out sleep-soup into bowls.

As he served, the mobsters sat at the long benches. None of them said thank you.

Drgnan had to still his beating heart to keep from trembling. He didn't want to think of what would happen if they detected the sleeping potion. They had a way of hanging people by their feet out windows. Then the ravens would come.

The lentil soup slid into bowls. *Slop. Slurp. Slugg. Slupp. Sock. Splotch. Splurch.*

While he served, the gangsters muttered to one another. ("I hope this don't have no cilantro in it. I hate that cilantro.") Drgnan Pghlik tried to not look at their eyes. He tried to show nothing. *Splurk. Splatch. Splunch.*

Only a few left to go.

Splutch. Splank. Splip.

And the last one. *Splock.*

He was done.

"Thank you," said the last gangster in line.

Drgnan Pghlik looked at the man in shock. None of them had ever said thank you.

He was a short, weasely sort of man. He looked at Drgnan with sudden interest.

Quickly Drgnan bowed and began to back out of the room with the empty vat.

"Not so fast," said the man. His name was Weasel Chops O'Reilly. He said, "I got a question for you."

Drgnan paused. Panic beat on the walls of his bare head. He tried to show nothing on his face. He clutched the vat to his chest like a baby, like a shield, like it would protect him. Within the tin, the ladle rocked.

The weasely man stepped forward. He said, "The boys hate cilantro. This got any cilantro in it?"

Drgnan breathed easily. "No," he said truthfully.

"You sure? 'Cause if there's cilantro, Bargain Basement McGhee is likely to flip his short stack, if you know what I mean, and start Pow! Pow! Pow!"

"There is no cilantro, sir," said Drgnan Pghlik.

"You sure?"

"I helped the cook make your dinner, sir. It is too delicious for gunplay."

"Says you. Let's give it the old dip-and-smack," said Weasel Chops, shoving his finger in his bowl and drawing it out, brown with lentils. He licked his finger. "Mm," he said. "Mm!"

Several more gangsters gave their soup a try.

"That is yummy," said Weasel Chops. "That is a high-class soup."

"Thank you, sir."

"Really."

"Thank you."

"Hits the spot."

"The Company of Saints smiles on your pleasure."

"So what are the ingredients?"

At that, Drgnan Pghlik froze. He didn't know what to say. He couldn't tell them what was in the soup.

"It is an old recipe," said Drgnan.

"I didn't ask if it was old," said the weasely man.

Now Drgnan Pghlik was terrified. He couldn't lie. He had taken a vow to never tell an untruth. "Just . . . in the soup . . . a lot of herbs and things. Simmered. On a fire."

"Come on. Share the secret," said the weasely man. "There's lentils. And carrots."

"And onions. And so on."

"So on?"

"So on."

"Naw. No so on."

"You know, so on."

"I say no so on. What's so on?"

"Ingredients."

"Yeah?"

"Yes, sir."

"Like?"

"Onions."

"You said that."

"Did I, sir?"

Weasel Chops smiled slowly. "You can't lie, can you?"

Sadly, Drgnan Pghlik said, "To lie is to duct-tape the eyes of the God of Fate. He still has hands to find you out and goose you."

"Yeah. So the complete list of ingredients. While I write them down on an index card so as I can send it to my mother, who is a great cook."

"I'm sure she is, sir," said Drgnan Pghlik with a sense of infinite sorrow. "I am sure that the feasts around the table of Mother Weasel Chops O'Reilly are spoken of in legend and song."

Weasel Chops O'Reilly had out his pen and an index card. "Go ahead, kid in a dress," he said. "Shoot."

Drgnan Pghlik could not lie—he had promised. He thought about a fib. But he knew he couldn't fib. He couldn't misrepresent. He couldn't tell a corker. He despaired of ever seeing his friends again. Everything was over. Solemnly, truthfully, he said: "Seven cups of lentils. Eighteen carrots. Ten onions, chopped. Thirty cups of water." He looked around the faces of the mobsters, all waiting. He finished: "Garlic. Bay leaves. Paprika. Chili powder. Bouillon. And a sleeping potion."

There was a stunned silence.

"Wow," one man said. "That's what gives it that extra zing, ain't it, boss?"

"Sleeping potion," Weasel Chops repeated grimly.

"Yes, sir," said Drgnan.

"You had a little plan, didn't you, kid?"

"Yes, sir."

Weasel Chops smiled. He strolled to the table, put down his index card. "I may leave off that last ingredient when my momma makes it."

"You might also want to cut the recipe down to a fourth," said Drgnan morosely. "Unless you're entertaining a larger company of sixteen to twenty people."

Weasel Chops lifted his soup. He held it level with his eyes. Steam laced his lashes and the monastery air. "A bowl of snooze chowder, huh?" he said. "You're a real cutup, kid. Think you're real cute, huh?" He walked over to Drgnan, lifted the vat out of Drgnan's arms, and handed Drgnan his own bowl.

"Eat up," he said. "You're off to Slumberland."

"What will you do with me, sir?"

"You'll see real soon."

"You will never triumph, sir," said Drgnan Pghlik. "There is no profit in evildoing."

"You think? I'll show you the receipts. Now take the spoon, and start plugging your whistle-hole, kid."

Drgnan Pghlik took his first bite of the soup. For a moment, Drgnan had the wild hope that maybe Weasel Chops had licked enough off his own index finger to knock him out cold—but no such luck. Even if Weasel Chops were to drop, there would still be nineteen more.

Helplessly Drgnan fed himself another

spoonful. And another. He was starting to get drowsy. The floor tipped.

"Feeling woozy?" said Weasel Chops. "Sweet dreams, kid in a dress. When you wake up, you're in for a little surprise."

Drgnan stumbled—the walls beat in and out around him.

Weasel Chops growled, "Think about this, kid, next time you decide to make alphabet soup with only the Zs."

Stone—in front of his eyes—the flagstone floor—and Drgnan couldn't move his arms—could feel the gangsters grab him—lifted—his head swung—he tried to fight—couldn't . . . move his . . . hands. . . .

Help! he thought. *Where is . . . help?*
Jasper! Jasper Dash!

Drgnan's old friend . . . best friend . . . Drgnan had gotten Jasper out of all kinds of scrapes: yeti—a lake of fire—attack ostriches—big gum . . . all sorts of . . . Yes, Jasper . . . Jasper Dash . . . Where . . . where was he?

And with his final waking breaths, Drgnan sent his mind out roving—spinning above the hurtling mountains, the frigid air, the billowy clouds . . . across the states, labeled as to capital, major rivers, imports and exports . . . across the nation . . .

To where Jasper Dash sat, staring at an opponent in the Pelt gymnasium . . .

HELP! JASPER DASH, I NEED YOUR HELP!

And then falling . . . darkness . . .

Drgnan Pghlik, brave young monk of Vbngoom, slept soundly.

19

It was not every day a wall collapsed at the Dupontville Fine Excellent View Stay Hotel.

It was every other day. The people who worked there were used to it. After a few days, most of the guests were used to it too.

"New balcony, honey," said one tourist to his wife through a hole in the wall.

She was in the bathroom on the john, reading a knitting magazine. "Nice," she said. "I never knew you could see the gutter factory from here."

"Yeah," said her husband, getting out his camera. He looked at the factory through the lens. He twiddled with some settings. "Autumn light on smokestacks," he muttered, "you ain't getting away from me now."

Meanwhile, the wreckage down below moved. A few pieces of concrete slid to the side. A door banged open. A cloud of dust puffed into the air.

Jasper Dash, Boy Technonaut, poked his head out and surveyed the wreckage. He was wearing a pith helmet.

From below him came a voice.

"Jasper?" said Katie. "Jasper? Am I alive?"

"I believe so," he replied. "Or if we are in Heaven, there are more mules than I imagined."

There were about four mules standing and looking at the pile of concrete and metal, wondering if there was anything there worth eating.

"Jasper?" said Katie's tinny, echoing voice. "Jasper, can we make an agreement to never, ever, ever use the Gyroscopic Sky Suite again?"

"I don't think we have to worry," said Lily, sticking her head out next to Jasper's. "It's crushed."

"Well, at least something good came out of this," said Katie, pulling herself out of the capsule, covered with brown dust. She slapped at her shirt and pants to get the grime out.

"Dash it all," said Jasper. "I guess we'll have to check into the hotel in the normal way."

"Ah," said Katie sarcastically. "You mean, instead of being fired from a rocket-launcher into the side of the hotel and having explosive clamps blow up and make a new doorway, we might just, I don't know, walk in and say, 'I'd like a room, please?'"

"Exactly," agreed Jasper.

"Well, that's a novel idea," said Katie.

"Sometimes, Katie," he replied, "new situations call for new solutions." He was already hopping down the chunks of concrete. Jasper wasn't very good at noticing sarcasm. And he was at his happiest after explosions.

Lily reached down and grabbed another pith helmet and scrambled after him, tottering on rubble. Katie shook her head and followed.

A secret policeman dressed in a suit too short for him and an old Tyrolean hat watched them go. He flipped open a little notepad and began writing.

Katie, Lily, and Jasper walked into the lobby of the hotel. There were some plastic chairs to sit in, most of them turned toward the wall, and a fountain that hadn't worked for years.

"Hello," said the proprietor, a paunchy man in a soccer shirt and flip-flops. He then spoke rapidly in a language Lily had never heard before that sounded like it might have roots in Eastern Europe, the planet Krypton, and a rock tumbler.

The three kids didn't know what to say.

In English the proprietor said, "You are not speak Doverian? You speak English?"*

The kids nodded.

"Okay, okay," said the man. "Welcome to Dupontville Fine Excellent View Stay Hotel. I can get you a room?"

---

*You may notice that the Delawarians in this book talk in kind of an irritating way.

We have to give them credit. English is not their first language. They speak a language peculiar to Delaware, unknown anywhere else, a rich tongue with its own poets and novelists and songwriters.

Before you make fun of them for the way they talk, answer me this: How much of *Delaware's* language do *you* speak, wise guy?

"Yes, please, sir," said Jasper. "One room with three beds."

The proprietor nodded. "Come, follow. Follow, follow." He took some keys off the desk and led the three kids up a flight of stairs. The hallway above was dark. There were rooms with numbers on the doors and a sound of rushing water. Lily was a bit worried about the sound of rushing water. She wondered when the ceiling was going to collapse.

The man rattled the keys in the lock of one room and threw the door open. "Very nice room," he said. "Very nice."

They looked in.

"Three beds," he said. "Television, chair, five coat hangers. Yes?"

"It's missing a wall," said Katie.

"Very nice view. Very nice view."

"Maybe we weren't specific enough," said Katie. "We'd like a room with three beds and at least four walls."

The man nodded and led them up another

flight of stairs. Here there was a light, but it flickered off whenever the wind in the broken window blew the dangling electrical cord back and forth through the puddle. He let them into another bedroom.

They looked around for a minute. There were three beds, four walls, and six coat hangers. Katie and Lily checked out the bathroom. Jasper went to the window and squinted out, calculating the sight lines for snipers.

"New bathroom, all modern amenities," said the proprietor.

"We'll take it," declared Jasper.

"There's a goat in the shower," said Katie.

"Very new goat," the man said. "Very good, nice goat."

"Yeah," said Katie, "but I don't think—"

Jasper asked gravely, "Do we have to feed it? Because if yes, I think you should take some off the nightly rate."

"Okay okay," said the proprietor. "I feed goat. If you stay long, you shave goat three times a year."

"It's a bargain, sir," said Jasper, holding out his hand.

They shook on it.

"Very good," said the proprietor.

Lily had walked over to one of the beds and pulled back the covers. "Um," she said, "this isn't a bed. It's four spies curled up with pillows on them."

"I am the foot of the bed," announced one of the spies.

"Look here," said Jasper. "That's just not right. We demand a real third bed."

"Okay okay," said the proprietor. "No spies. Cot instead by tonight. We will put up cot here." He spoke in rapid Doverian to the four spies. He jerked his thumb. Three of them got up and shamefacedly filed toward the door.

"And you," said Jasper to the last one.

"I cannot move," said the spy. He stayed hunkered on the floor.

One of the men by the door said, "Mrglik, his leg is fall asleep."

"We will have Mrglik remove," said the proprietor. "No problem, children. No worry."

"Gone by tonight?" said Jasper.

"Gone by tonight. Okay?"

"Fine."

"Okay." The proprietor smiled and nodded. "Good. You need anything—tea, coffee, sheet, room service, police—you just say so near the painting of friendly clown here."

"Thank you."

"Speak slow, though, please. Sometimes it not work so good."

So they had a room for the night. Now it was time to go out and find a guide—and explore the ancient and exotic streets of Dover!

20

Lily's first real view of the city was overwhelming. So many things were happening at once that she couldn't take it all in: Goats wandered in the mud and broken blacktop of the street, and chickens, too, strutting in the dirty bushes, and three-wheeled cars swerved around stray dogs and honked, and there were schoolkids dressed in tunics and smiley-faced masks, and men with baskets of roots, and bicycle carts painted red and green and yellow, in the backseats of which women in tiaras and lipstick reclined and yelled into cell phones. Blond barbarians, mercenary warriors from Hazzard Landing, from Broadkill and Slaughter Beaches, shoved their way through the crowds, swords strapped to their oiled backs, while priests of mystery religions peered out from behind their veils and crept into alleys. There were girls in their *blrga*-shirts and *pochbtvms*, traditional dress of Dover (*see illus.*), buying snacks from an old man with snakes around his shoulders. Old women almost bent double stumbled along with broken televisions tied to their backs with twine. Cattle lowed. Sheep bleated. Cologne salesmen walked to and fro with huge atomizers, puffing scent on men who staggered under burdens of bricks, and ladder peddlers carried their wares on their head, nearly knocking down tall men every time they looked both ways to cross the road.

Lily was thrilled by all of it. She couldn't take it all in. It was like breathing with her eyes. She didn't always like what she saw, but she was glad she was seeing it.

"What language are they speaking?" asked Lily.

"Doverian," said Jasper. "It is deuced hard to learn. I do not mind telling you that the pronunciation is the absolute dickens. Since the beginning of the Autarch's despotic rule, the state has been too poor for many vowels."

"Do you speak it?" said Lily.

"No, I'm afraid not. I was silent for that year in Vbngoom. But I know it is a language of great poetic beauty."

"It sounds like someone being kicked off a cliff," said Katie grumpily. "And I mean a cliff with metal railings."

They walked through the muddy streets. In the shadow of the huge, blackened concrete towers, mules pulled carts, and people had made fire-pits, where they cooked meat and noodles for sale. Laundry dried on electrical wires.

One of the tusked, six-armed warriors of far Lumbrook stood lolling against a wall, rattling one of his many hands around in a bag of Doritos. He watched lazily as they passed.

The city of Dover had sparkled, Jasper

explained, before the coming of the Autarch. But he stole from the poor to give to the rich; and now there were many things broken, and few things whole.

The three stopped to get some lunch, sitting on huge pieces of concrete and drinking noodle slurries out of old margarine containers. Though the surroundings were grim, the food was very cheap and was tasty, too.

"What are those spoons on some of the rooftops?" asked Lily.

"Those aren't spoons," said Jasper. "They're an ancient form of transportation in this state. Vaultapults. Commuter catapults. You get into one, an attendant points you in the right direction, pulls the vaultapult back, and sends you flying to the roof of the right building."

"That seems kind of dangerous," said Katie.

"People here are used to it by long custom," said Jasper. "Still, it is not easy to land without harm. It takes a keen eye, a quick leg, and springy ankles. I used the vaultapults occasionally at Vbngoom, but they still worry me. For example,

I hope that I shall never have to use vaultapults during a high-speed chase by night over the rooftops of Dover."

"So that's what I saw on top of that model the Delawarians were selling to Mr. Lecroix from the museum," said Katie.

"Indeed," said Jasper. "Humble though that model may be, it is one of the few representations of Vbngoom and was made by a great master in the art of scissors and taping."

They each slurped more noodle slurry and picked up cabbage with their tongs, looking up to the patch of sky between buildings as bodies hurled through the air from catapult to catapult, some dragging bundles of cloth, baskets of candles, or sheep with them as they flew. It was a fascinating sight.

Just as they were finishing their meal, they heard a cry of, "Look at the little dears!" It did not sound very Doverian. They glanced up to see a woman dressed in jeans, duck boots, a head scarf, and a brand-new *blrga*-shirt. She was peering down at them. She had clapped her hand to her throat and was saying, "Poor little things . . . Little Delawarians. What's—your—name? Do—you—speak—English?"

"I am Jasper Dash, Boy Technonaut."

"My—name—is—Lisa—Buldene. I—am—from—New—York—City." More to herself than to Jasper, she said, "Poor thing. It looks like no one's given you new clothes since 1943. Here," she said, reaching into her bag. "Take—some—candy—bars."

"Great," said Katie. "Thanks."

"While we appreciate your kindness," said Jasper, "we cannot possibly accept a gift of candy while our toothbrushes are buried under so much rubble."

"You speak English beautifully!" the woman said.

"Thanks," said Katie, tearing into a candy bar and chomping. "I been studifying real hard."

"Oh," explained Lily softly, "we're not Doverians. We're just visiting from another state."

"Aha!" The woman laughed, covering her

forehead with her hand. "Oh, I'm sorry! I thought you were small Delawarian orphans with bright shining eyes! What a silly mistake." She sat down beside them. "How long have you been here? Don't you just love it?" she asked. Before Lily could respond, the woman continued, "I mean, wow, I just feel so fulfilled. Every day I'm having new experiences. I've seen all these palaces and temples and museums, and I've gone to all these bazaars, and yesterday I had a real interview with the secret police, and they were really nice and interested in me and everything I had to say. Then later this guy—oh, one sec." She waved to a street vendor, who rolled his rattling cart and umbrella over. She ordered some kind of chicken sausage.

The man shrugged, pointed to his mouth and his ear, and said apologetically, "Has no English. No English."

Lisa Buldene whispered to the kids, "I love how they talk here. It's so quaint and darling. You can tell they're a very simple, basic people."

She shouted a few words in broken Doverian

that, translated into English, would be something like, *Me want to has the thicken.*

The sausage salesman's eyes winced with uncertainty. *The thicken?* he asked.

She jabbed a finger at the chicken. *Thicken! Thicken!* she demanded.

The man smiled and responded in Doverian, *Ah, madam, indeed, I see! You mean one of my fine chicken-dogs. Superlative. I believe you will find it to your taste, zesty with spices culled in the hanging gardens of Eberton. The meat is rich with drippings.* He served her a sausage wrapped in flatbread. *You speak Doverian?* he asked her.

Me sauce, she answered, pointing. He gave her some ketchup. She handed him a big, messy wad of cash. He looked at it in surprise. Then he tipped his cap, looked at her like she was crazy, and strolled away with his cart, shaking his head.

"Wasn't he a cute old guy? They're all so beautiful. They have such lovely souls." Lisa Buldene held the sausage up to her nose to breathe in its steam. She exclaimed, "What do you think this sauce is?

I've had so many exotic things to eat here in the last few days, I'm kind of in this great foodie haze. Everything I've been served is just fab. I cannot even tell you. Yesterday I had these disks of meat that had been frozen, you know, to lock in all their ancient goodness, and then thrown on a grill and fried, and . . . Wow. Wow, this sauce smells heavenly. I wonder what it is! Just imagine the little girls in their hats and bells mashing it up in some village courtyard and singing to their donkey!"

"Um," said Lily, "I think it might be regular ketch—"

"I am completely filled up to here with glory," sighed Lisa Buldene. "The people here are just so *authentic*, so *spiritual*. I've gotten to know so many new people. . . . Like you, for example. At home, in New York, I wouldn't have even talked to you, but here we are, exchanging opinions and—"

"Saturn's moons!" cried Jasper. "There's the van!"

"That's not really an opinion," said Lisa. "It's more like an exclamation, but I feel that way the whole time here, too, like exclaiming, like crying out to the world that—"

Jasper had stood, dropped his margarine bowl and tongs, and set off running.

Because he had just seen a white van drive past—filled with the fake Delaware Stare-Eyes champions!

21

"What van?" asked Lisa Buldene. She saw the three kids had scampered away: Jasper first, Katie close behind, and then Lily running as fast as she could. *"What van?"* the New Yorker called after them. *"Is this something I should see? Is it in your guidebook?"* She rummaged in her big bag and pulled out her *There and Back Again™ Guide to Greater Delaware* and began flipping through its index wildly.

The van rattled down the rutted street. Chickens scurried out of its way. Women with baskets on their heads leaped onto stoops.

The three friends charged after it. They followed it around a corner—and found themselves in a little cobbled square where a work crew of spavined centaurs was dragging stone blocks. The square was crowded with the half-human, half-horse construction workers; the kids couldn't see the van at all in the crowd of horse legs and granite. But they heard the van's engine rev.

"There!" shouted Katie, and began dodging her way through the centaurs.

Jasper watched her with wide eyes. He saw something she didn't see. "NO, KATIE!" he screamed. "NOOOO!"

But Katie didn't hear him.

22

"NO, KATIE!"

This time, Katie heard his yell—stopped in her tracks—and looked back, tottering. Jasper was racing toward her.

"You almost jaywalked!" he called. "Don't worry! I see a designated crosswalk just ahead of you!"

"Jasper!" she snarled, and took off again.

He puffed up along beside her. "If we become like our enemies, then we have lost!"

She rolled her eyes. "Yeah. And if we lose our enemies, what then?" They barreled down a street and leaped over a stream.

The van disappeared around a bend near a lopsided old brick building with ancient heroes carved on its doorway. By the time Jasper and

Katie got there, they couldn't tell which way it had gone.

"Great," said Katie. "Thanks."

"I'll go this way; you and Lily go that," said Jasper, hurtling off down the road.

Katie waved back to Lily and took off in the other direction.

She ran out into a square with some kind of lumpy monument in the center surrounded by sick grass. The van was on the other side, trundling away down the street. Katie looked back quickly to make sure that Lily had seen her. Lily, puffing along behind, was waving her hands and looked like she was trying to say something. Lily wasn't a very fast runner. Katie didn't have time to stop; the van was already a couple of blocks away. She plunged onward.

They were passing down a row of cloth shops with samples in bright colors hung up for sale on the street. Merchants sat on wide beds and drank tea. When the van roared past, the cloth samples rose up and flapped as if scolding.

Katie slipped in a mud hole and fell—hit her knee—got back up and kept running. The van was just a little farther away now. She could see one of the kids from the team looking out of the back window at her.

"Katie!" Lily's voice came from far behind her. Katie barreled forward.

The van slid along the row of shops—turned to the left—leaving behind clouds of gray smoke.

Katie followed.

The van turned right—passed over a bridge. Katie, her breath heaving, her heart pounding, followed—just in time to see the van screech to a halt at a crossroad. A procession of the city's Investment Bankers' Guild was marching to their temple with money-green banners and fanfares from bugle and drum.

There were a lot of them.

Ha, thought Katie. The van couldn't move an inch.

She walked up slowly toward it. She felt triumphant. They weren't going to escape now. She crossed her arms, smiled an arch smile, and strolled right behind the Stare-Eyes team.

But now something occurred to her. Maybe it was the thing Lily had been shouting about.

She didn't really know what to do, now that she had caught the van. She realized suddenly that she was supposed to follow it *secretly.* Instead of walking right up behind it. And watching its door slide open. And having about eight heads poke out and look right at her.

Whoops, thought Katie, stopping in her tracks. *I really should have thought this through earlier.*

Eight boys stared back at her. And they were really good at staring.

23

"It's that *girl*," said one of the boys. "The one from Pelt."

Team Mom stuck her head out the door. "Katie Mulligan," she said. "From Horror Hollow. We've been introduced."

"Oh," said Katie weakly. "Hi."

In front of the van, the procession of investment bankers continued, bearing ornate piggy banks that sloshed with spare change at every step.

One of the boys gestured to Katie. "You wanted to catch us," he said through his toothy mouth. "Here we are."

"Get in," another invited.

"Yeah," said Team Mom. "Get in, Katie M. We're all waiting."

"There's room in the back," a boy said.

"Could I . . . could I just get your autographs?"

"This isn't about autographs," said Team Mom. "This is about guts. Guts and glory."

"Ummmm," said Katie. "Could I just get a double order of glory?"

The procession in front of the van had passed. The music was already fading.

"We'll meet again, Katie," said Team Mom. "Believe me. And I'll fork out for a double order of guts. Yours."

The van rolled forward through the intersection.

Soon it was gone.

24

Katie and Lily trudged back along the street of silk merchants. On the crumbling brick walls, pasted up next to ancient carved window frames, were posters of the Awful and Adorable Autarch of Dagsboro. He had huge, piratical mustaches that pointed up at each end. He wore big, square plastic glasses that would have looked dumb even back in the eighties, when they were from, and an ugly necktie. The poster was covered with slogans in Doverian. To deface one of the posters—by removing the ridiculous mustaches, for example, rubbing out the goatee, erasing the stupid glasses, or whiting out the missing tooth—was punishable by death. Katie and Lily strolled right by his idiotic gaze.

Katie said, "You were telling me not to let them see me, weren't you?"

Lily shrugged.

"Okay, I get it," said Katie. "Next time, I'll listen. I'm sorry. It's just that Jasper stopped me in the middle of the chase to yell about crosswalks or buckle up for safety or something. So you yelled and I wasn't into the halt."

When they found Jasper, he was walking toward them with a young man in a T-shirt and rubber shoes.

"No luck, chums?" asked Jasper.

Katie told him what had happened. Jasper listened attentively.

"No matter, Katie. More important: I have located a guide. This is Bntno."

Bntno put his hands over his eyes in a traditional Delawarian sign of respect. He said, "I shall lead the dandy children to the mountains."

"I have to follow the same route I went last time," Jasper explained to him. "We must seek four mountains. One with a lake on it, one with a glacier on it, one with a pine forest on it, and one with a pillar of stone on it. The monastery is on one of those four peaks."

"I know this mountains. I love this glacier. I have spoked with this pillar for days. These places, they are to me as familiar as my own back."

"Super," said Jasper.

"You don't know your own back at all," said Katie. "No one sees their own back."

"Maybe I have seen it in the mirror. Just as we see all things in a mirror."

"Maybe," said Katie.

"Maybe when I go to the shop and try on shirts."

"Okay," said Katie.

"It is very dangerous journey," said Bntno.

"We are determined as steel," said Jasper.

"Very good," said Bntno. "Then tomorrow I come to your hotel at six. We leaves early."

"Early," agreed Jasper.

The young man once again put his hands over

his eyes in the gesture of respect and then backed away. He slammed into a dentist.

"Do you think he really knows what he's talking about?" said Katie. "I don't want us to get lost."

"He will get us as far as those mountains," said Jasper. "It's important to have faith in people, Katie."

"Hmm," said Katie.

Bntno had just run into a telephone pole.

25

They ate dinner at a restaurant where the six-armed tribesmen of the north performed acrobatic dances and traditional wailing-songs until you paid them to go away. For a dollar and fifty-five cents each, Lily, Jasper, and Katie got rice, vegetable medley, and a meat puck. A sign on the wall said in English, ASK ABOUT OUR DELICHIOUS DEEP-FRIED DRGSL MOUNTAIN SQUID! ONE TENTACLE, IT SERVE YOU *AND* YOUR HONEY-BUNNEY SWEETHEAT!

No one was asking about the deep-fried Drgsl mountain squid. For one thing, they were too busy ducking while the six-armed, tusked dancing girls did high kicks for small change.

At a quiet moment, when Lily could be heard

over the nose-harps and tusk-plucked goo-tars, she asked Jasper, "What, um, what are we going to be looking for with Bntno?"

"Vbngoom lies hidden in a mountain range in northern Delaware, where the cruel ice still clings to the slopes. There are four mountains in this hidden range. It was at the base of these four mountains that I, stung by the killer bees and hunted by the counterfeiting ring, passed out beneath a banyan tree. When I woke up, I had been spirited away to Vbngoom, which lies on the top of one of these mountains."

"Can't you remember which mountain?" asked Katie.

"No. I was unconscious, Katie, and all I know is that the temple lies atop one of the four peaks. No mortal knows which. And it is said that these mountains, in deep mist, switch places to keep their secret hidden, so that no prying eyes can view the monastery."

"Well, clearly," said Katie, "some mortals know about it now."

"Yes," said Jasper. "Unfortunately so."

"The Stare-Eyes team."

"Exactly."

"And Bntno. If he really knows anything."

"Indeed."

Now village dancers of the six-armed race of the north were performing complicated hurls and spins, all their arms wheeling. Jasper and Katie were seated with their backs to them, but Lily could see their incredible bounding, the swivel of their tusked heads, the clapping and twirling. She was dazzled. She could feel the rhythm in her ankles.

"Hello," said Katie. "Earth to Lily. Come in, Lills."

Lily didn't want to tear her eyes away from all the eight-limbed whirling. "It's beautiful," she said.

Katie turned around and looked for a second. She shook her head. "I get motion sickness too easy."

Pulling herself back from the dance, Lily

asked Jasper, "What can you remember about the mountains?"

"Only what I told you before. That there were four of them: one with a lake, one with a pine forest, one with a huge stone pillar covered in ancient writing, and one with a glacier that never melted."

"What are they called?" asked Katie. "We can get a map."

"They have names not pronounceable by mortals."

"That's really inconvenient," said Katie. She took a bite and wiggled her fork around. "Oh, and hey. Explain to us about these secret powers that the Stare-Eyes team got."

"At the center of Vbngoom are pits where sacred flames burn. No one without special training and great humility is allowed to go near them. Monks who have meditated by these flames acquire special powers. They can levitate and speak with their minds. I fear the boys from the Stare-Eyes team have been exposed illegally to these flames."

"So they're kind of becoming a powerful force of supernatural evil?"

"I am afraid so, Katie."

"That would explain why the bugs in Pelt went crazy when they appeared."

"I fear for the Stare-Eyes players themselves, as well as for us. It is dangerous to get close to those flames without years of training. I worry they are being pushed by Team Mom and their coach to acquire powers that might destroy them."

"So why don't the monks stop them from going to the sacred flames?"

"Most of the monks of Vbngoom have taken an oath of nonviolence. Only a few, like my friend Drgnan Pghlik, have learned the ways of martial arts so that they can protect the monastery. I suspect the art-thieving gang has complete control of Vbngoom at this point."

Lily heard the discussion, but she was looking past them. She watched the six-armed men and women weave patterns in the air, tapestries of muscle and sinew that had been braided on the looms of ten centuries, and she imagined herself as a little six-armed goat-girl, high in the steppes of the Newark Mountains, playing her Pan-flutes, and her fiddle, and her drum, and her finger-cymbals, all at once. She imagined herself learning these ancient dances, wearing rough clothes of yak's wool and ogre skin—and maybe there would be a six-armed boy with a knowledge of all the old epics of their kind who would look shyly at her, and she would see him from the hilltop, and wave, and wave, and wave, and wave, and wave, and—

The waiter appeared at their side. "Everything good?" he asked. "Let me to fix the reception." He adjusted the knife and fork on the fourth placemat. "We can't hear good what you are saying." He looked toward the kitchen.

A man in a black suit gave him a thumbs-up.

The waiter nodded and said, "Much better, friends. Speak loud and not too near ashtray. You would like more mixed veg?"

26

Drgnan Pghlik awoke from his heavy slumber. He opened his eyes, and found that there was nothing to see. Everything was dark.

At first, he thought he was still asleep. His head was filled with outlines and blurs. He moved his hand across his face. He felt his nose, his mouth. He held his hand an inch from his eyes. Nothing. Absolutely black.

Carefully he swiped his hands through the air. He reached for the floor beneath him. It was made of stone. It was dusty. He ran the heel of his hand along through the grit. He found the bottom of a wooden door.

He walked his fingers up the slats until he found the handle. He rattled it.

Locked. He was locked in. "Hello?" he called. "Hello?"

There was no answer.

He reached out in the other direction. Fumbling in the air, he felt a wide, empty space . . . then . . . cardboard. He felt a stack of thin, cardboard boxes.

Slowly light dawned in his woozy, confused brain. He realized that he was locked in the closet where they stored board games. Board games and . . . He couldn't remember what else. Board games and . . .

"Hello?" he called, even louder this time.

Things shifted in the darkness around him. He pulled himself up against the door.

A light went on in the next room. There was a line of light under the door. Drgnan bobbed his head down and pressed it against the cool floor, trying to see what was in the next room.

Shoes. The soles of black shoes.

"The kid's awake," said a gangster in the next room.

The door briefly unlocked. Two men stood there. They shoved a bowl at him and slammed the door. He heard them turning the key in the lock.

He put the bowl on his lap. He reached in. Something smooshy . . . Some kind of thick paste. Wet.

He picked up a handful. He held it up near his nose.

It was raw hamburger.

He dropped it back in the bowl.

"I shall not eat this," he announced through the door. "I do not believe in eating the flesh of animals."

"You hear that?" said one of the gangsters. "Kid in a dress don't believe in eating the flesh of animals."

"Okay. Okay. Kid in a dress: You want we should take it away?" asked the other.

"Take it if you want," said Drgnan Pghlik darkly. "You shall never make me eat it."

"Hokey-dokey, girly blokey." The keys rattled.

Something dimly registered in the back of Drgnan's brain.

The door opened again—the gangster stooped down, grabbed the bowl, and slammed the door shut.

This time Drgnan heard that not all of the shuffling motion was on the other side of the door.

Something was in the closet with him.

"Hello?" he said again, quietly.

There was a deep, bass growl. A growl so slow, so low, he could hear the spaces between its *R*s.

And then he realized: He knew where he was. He knew what was in the dark with him.

He was in the closet where they stored the board games and the monastery tiger.

That raw hamburger meat hadn't been for him.

"It's a real shame," said the gangster, "that the tiger's food is outside of the closet. See, 'cause the tiger, he's *in* the closet, and he ain't eaten in a few days."

Awful. Drgnan Pghlik slapped his hand to his forehead.

His sticky hand.

"And it's even more of a shame," said the gangster, "that you handled his grub. Because now you probably smell like fresh meat."

Drgnan Pghlik had romped with the tiger when he was a small tot. He had fed him, on occasion, in the years since. He knew that when the tiger was hungry, nothing would stop him from pouncing. The tiger was dangerous. He called softly, "Nrrrgarha? Nrrrgarha, boy?"

There was an answering growl. The tiger shifted in the shadows.

"You won't eat me, boy, will you?"

The tiger stood. The tiger paced to Drgnan's side. The tiger sniffed at Drgnan's wet palm and wet forehead.

The tiger growled again.

"Naw, he won't eat you," said the gangster. "Not today. You know, he might even cuddle up to you. For old time's sake. Auld lang syne."

"Tomorrow," said the other gangster. "Now tomorrow is a whole different story."

"Tomorrow he might commence to getting a little peckish. He might commence to getting a little bite-y. In fact, I won't be any surprised if the claws come out tomorrow."

The tiger sniffed at Drgnan's hand. The tiger growled louder.

Jasper, thought Drgnan Pghlik. *Jasper Dash, I hope you're on your way.*

Nrrrgarha drew long breaths and pictured corned beef.

27

It turned out that Lisa Buldene was staying at the same hotel as our heroes. They met her at the roof-top restaurant that evening when they sat in plastic garden chairs, watching people get flung through the sky from vaultapults as the clouds turned red with sunset. The tiny little bodies hurtled, catching the light for a few instants before the arc of their motion brought them back down upon another rooftop. Slowly, wearily, people migrated home from their jobs, briefcases flapping, to make dinner over their gas rings or cook-fires.

"What are you drinking?" Lisa Buldene asked Katie, sitting down beside her.

Katie looked at the label. "The state-sponsored cola. Yum. 'Tyrant Splash.'" She took a big swig.

"Sure," said Lisa Buldene, smiling. "I tried it earlier. But it's actually not a cola. It's the Delaware government's brand of bottled water. Straight from the St. Jones River."

"What do you mean?" said Katie. "It sure tastes like a cola. And it's brown and bubbly. And fizzes. And . . . um . . . So it's really . . . ?"

Lisa Buldene nodded.

Katie's face kind of dropped. She ran for the railing of the balcony and began spitting up.

"So did you catch your van today?" Lisa Buldene asked Lily and Jasper. "I looked it up in my *There and Back Again,* and the only vanlike thing they had was a cart that carries the god of traffic through the major intersections of the city at noon on Fridays to pray for no gridlock."

"That is not the van in question," said Jasper. "This is a different van."

"We have our own private van situation," said Katie from the railing.

"Where are you off to next?" Lisa Buldene asked. "You decided?"

"Vbngoom, the Platter of Heaven," said Katie. Jasper hissed in warning.

Lisa Buldene gasped. "Oh, break my heart! You're not! You're going to Vbngoom? I thought no one could find it! I haven't even been able to find a postcard of it! My *There and Back Again* says it moves all the time."

"It's in the guidebook?" said Jasper.

"Yeah, sure. Everything's in my *There and Back Again.*" She opened her bag, ducked her head inside, and reemerged with a guidebook. She handed it to Jasper, who began flipping through it.

The New Yorker watched him, slouched in her seat. "Do you think you've seen the *real* Delaware yet?" she asked. "I mean, we all hear the stories—you know, the camels, the temples, the jewels, the snakes with women's heads, the women with snakes' heads, that whole thing—but I'm saying, sometimes I go to all the places it says to go in my *There and Back Again,* all the places where it says you can see the real, authentic Delaware, and then I get there, and there are just these fifteen other tourists standing there in the courtyard of that castle or that particular volcanic crater, looking around with their fingers stuck in their own copies of *There and Back Again.*" Lisa Buldene looked very tense. "Then I get really worried I'm not actually seeing the real Delaware at all, and that maybe there isn't a real Delaware anymore, because it's all just set up for tourists now. We can't see it because we know too much what to expect from the *There and Back Again.* No place is real anymore."

Jasper read aloud, with interest—and then increasing disgust, "'Vbngoom has been the most secret of the hidden mountain monasteries for centuries. Currently located on top of scenic Mount Tlmp, it offers great views, cheap meals, comfy lodging'—*comfy lodging?*—'private bathrooms, and eternal life. When you've made it to Vbngoom, you know you've made it to someplace unique.'"

"See?" said Lisa Buldene. "That's why I want to get to Vbngoom. Not because they have eternal life. But because I know it's still real and untouched. Hardly any other tourists have been there. If I got there, I would know I was really living—you know, *living*. Myself."

"But Vbngoom is in the guidebook too," said Lily.

Lisa Buldene wasn't listening. "A *real* place is the thing everyone searches for," she continued, her voice full of yearning. "You can't know yourself until you go someplace unknown. And what if there's no place unknown left?" She stood up, clearly unhappy. "I'm sorry, I've got to go," she said, close to tears. "My *chakras* are twingeing."

"Are you okay?" asked Lily.

Lisa Buldene picked up Katie's bottle of Tyrant Splash from the little glass-topped table. "You going to drink the rest of this?" she asked Katie. "Because if you aren't, I am." She declared tearfully, "This is the only way I can really get the state of Delaware inside of me." She drank a big gulp of the fizzy waters of the St. Jones.

"Delaware!" she whispered. "You're on my tongue now!" With that, she walked off.

Jasper called after her, "Ma'am, your guidebook!" but she was gone.

Soon after dinner, the three went to their room to go to bed, since they had to get up early. They brushed their teeth and Katie washed out her mouth with every liquid they had brought with them: water, ginger ale, toothpaste, peroxide, and Jasper's foot ointment. Then they got into their beds and lay there in the dark, waiting for sleep.

"Lisa Buldene is weird," said Katie. "Of course stuff is real. You can knock it." She knocked on the wall.

"I cannot believe," Jasper complained bitterly, "that this guidebook just straight-up tells you the name of the mountain. Mount Tlmp. Like that!"

"I kind of know what Lisa Buldene is talking about, though," said Lily quietly. "Once, when I was a little kid, I really wanted to go to Sloth Dent National Park. You know, out west. It's that place where a giant sloth that lived in the Pleistocene era stopped moving for about three months. It, you know, fell asleep. So it left an impression in the mud. You can still see it today, one million years later. I really, really wanted to go. I looked at books about it and postcards, and I dreamed of lying there at night in the park, seeing this ancient sloth print under the stars. I thought all about fast-moving time and slow-moving sloths ... and finally one year we went ... "

"And what happened?" Katie asked.

"I don't know. I didn't really care once we got there. The park didn't look surprising. It just looked like all the photos I'd seen a million times."

"Which is like what?"

Lily shrugged. "A big sloth print."

"Just a footprint?"

"Well, no, the sloth was hanging upside down from a tree the whole time. So it's a back print."

"A back print."

"Yeah."

"A big, really hairy sloth back print?"

"Yeah. That was all."

Katie nodded. "Huh," she said. She sucked in her lips. She kept nodding. "Yeah, I can see why that would be kind of a disappointment."

"Not as much of a disappointment," said Jasper, "as seeing that a secret monastery is listed in a travel guide as having 'comfy lodging.'" He lay the guidebook beside him on the nightstand. "Well, good night, fellows."

"Good night," said Lily.

"Good night, Jasper," said Katie.

"Good night, Katie," said Jasper. "Good night, Lily."

"Good night, Lily," said Katie.

"Jasper," said Lily, "did you just put that book down on the nightstand?"

"Yes, Lily. Do you want it?"

"No, Jasper. Um, I was just thinking: There isn't any nightstand in this room."

She was right. There was no nightstand.

Suddenly everyone's feet got very cold.

The There and Back Again™

Guide to GREATER ~DELAWARE

Your passport to the Blue Hen State!
The most exotic of the Mid-Atlantic States lies open before you!

- **Eat Your Fill** after reading our chapter on cuisine. Try indigenous delicacies: Sip a hamster-milk smoothie, slice into a -12 oz. cloud steak in high Elsmere, or sup at the generous spittle-vats of Gumboro.

- **Go Off the Beaten Track** with our chapter on adventure vacations! Ride the monster-infested rapids of Dragon Creek through the canyons of the Pulaski Forest. Trek up the glaciers of the Newark Steppe and see the frost newts hiss ice at the sun.

- **Catch *Very Few* of Delaware's Disfiguring Diseases** with our chapter on health and safety! Avoid humblethroat, squank, the blue tussles, and Ponxwll's knee (at least types D and H)!

- **Make Out Like a Bandit** with our chapter on shopping! Haunt the bazaars of Dover and come back to your hotel, heavy-laden with *birga*-shirts, marionettes, knee-pads, and rare spices. Load your sand-tortoises high with gems and brasswork from the desert of the west, the caravanserai of Sandtown, and thrilling Whiteleysburg. Then meet real, actual bandits on Route 95! Give them everything! Quickly.

- **Relax in Splendor** with our chapter on lodging! From your hotel balcony, watch the winged mansions and hovering heli-burbs of Elsmere eclipse the rice terraces far below. Or stay at one of the submarine resorts of Seaford, often called "the Venice of Delaware." Speak too openly against the dictator, and spend years in one of Wilmington Castle's dungeons!

- **Speak the Language Like a Native** with our chapter on useful travel phrases! Learn how to say everything from "Please send this back to the kitchen" to "I will tell you anything! Just cage the sharks!"

- **Avoid Travel Hassles** with our chapter on Delaware's travel policies and laws. Always smile broadly when questioned by the police or spies! Never look anyone in the eye! Don't say anything important near shrubs!

"With the *There and Back Again Guide to Greater Delaware* in my rucksack, my family had a great trip—and half of us made it back out!"
—Rick Dubois, satisfied customer

There and Back Again™ Travel Guides: The Adventure Isn't Over Until After It Begins. ©

28

Jasper reached over and switched on the light.

"Mrglik!" he cried to the nightstand. "You're supposed to be gone!"

"Oh, yes?" said the spy. "Oh, forgot! Forgot! I am so sorry. I am so sorry, little man. Heh. Heh. Will instantly vamoose." He stood and began to shuffle sideways toward the door.

"Leave the lamp and the book!" Jasper ordered.

Shamefaced, Mrglik removed the lamp and the book from his head and handed them to Katie. He bowed awkwardly, straightened his black tie, and walked to the door. "Good night, peoples," he said. He opened the door, excused himself to step by a muscley kid in a tracksuit with a gun whose hand was on the doorknob, and walked away down the hall.

Mrglik walked down the three flights of concrete stairs while, from above, came the sounds of shots, screams, and the shattering of glass.

When Mrglik got to the lobby, he bowed to the proprietor, who was sitting on the rim of the broken fountain, cracking cashews with his teeth. The proprietor said good night to him and said he'd see him in the morning, ha ha, unless Mrglik's disguise was too devilishly clever. Mrglik always appreciated a compliment, and smiled widely, walking onward with a little spring in his step.

He left the hotel and climbed over the huge heap of rubble and the broken Sky Suite, continuing down past the public fountain and the dark, marble temple of Yyuhoo,* lit with flaring torches. Eventually he reached the Ministry of

---

*The Delawarian love goddess. As tweed-clad British world explorer Lesley Arbuckle-Smythe notes in his volume on Delaware, *Five Years in the Land of the Blue Hen:* "Just as the Delawarians save their ornament and their precious metals to adorn their temples, so do they show the wealth and opulence of their gods by lavishing upon them all the vowels—*A, E, I, O, U,* and sometimes *Y*—that are so desperately absent from the rest of the language. Hence we hear of Auimeu, father of the gods; Oouquoo, god of balanced justice; Yyuhoo, goddess of love; YoUDee, the Blue Hen herself; and at the most extreme, Aiiieee, the fearsome god of war."

Silence's secret underground lair. It was in an old bowling alley with a very nice painted sign that said, MINISTRY OF SILENCE, UNDERGROUND LAIR DIVISION. They did not have enough money to actually put the division underground.

He knocked, called out, "It is Mrglik!" and his friend Lknosz opened the door.

Inside there were desks set up on the bowling lanes, lit by whatever lamps people could bring from home. Mrglik went over to his boss's desk. His boss had brought in his daughter's Winnie the Pooh lamp. Pooh was holding on to a bunch of balloons and his feet were in the air. In an effort to make the lamp a little more menacing, Mrglik's boss had written a word bubble in Doverian, coming out of Pooh's mouth, that said, "Aha, enemies of the state! From this height I have perfect view of your illegal activities!"

"Report?" said Mrglik's boss, not looking up, turning over carbon pages in a file folder.

"They are going to Vbngoom, the Platter of Heaven."

"Excellent," said Mrglik's boss. He tried saying

it again, this time more evil. "Exxxcellent."

"I should mention, Impressive Superior, that they are most likely dead. As I left the room, there appeared to be an athlete with a gun."

"He wished to kill them?"

"So it appeared, Dazzling Mentor."

"Hmm," mused Mrglik's boss, rattling his fingers on his desk. He asked sharply, "JV or varsity?"

"Sir?"

"The athlete."

"The light was dim, sir."

"Sit," said Mrglik's boss. "We shall discuss a strategy."

They talked about how they might proceed. How they might find out from the kids where the secret monastery lay, and take it over for the good of His Most Terrifying Majesty the Autarch, so His Majesty might use its powers to crush all enemies of the state. Those three kids were the key. If, indeed, the three kids were still alive after their encounter with that armed athlete.

Having met for a while with his boss, Mrglik

went home to relax. There was nothing Mrglik liked more than a quiet night in. While the bustle and excitement of spying were enjoyable, as far as they—

I'm sorry, you seem to be impatient. Is there something you want to know about?

Let me look around the room. Oh, I'm the one telling the story. So sit tight, Bucky Jones, and see what comes your way.

After meeting for a while with his boss, Mrglik went home to relax. He took off his black shoes and flexed his stocking feet on his glass table. He turned on the television. There was only one station, the official government station, and tonight was *The Adorable Autarch's Hit Parade.* It was a popular program, but that was just because it was the only program on television. It was His Terrifying Majesty, the Awful and Adorable Autarch of Dagsboro, singing pop songs of the 1990s, live. When Mrglik turned on the set, His Majesty was finishing a high-pitched cover of "Dreamlover." Then followed "My Heart Will Go On" and "(I'm Missing You Like) Candy."

Mrglik eventually had to go to the toilet, but he could not get up because the Awful and Adorable Autarch was still singing, and Mrglik knew his spy friend Ttfrumpt was behind a two-way mirror, watching to see if Mrglik missed one exciting moment of the Autarch's performance. If Mrglik left the room, Ttfrumpt would report it. So Mrglik crossed his legs, and behind the mirror, Ttfrumpt, who also had to go to the toilet but couldn't because he had to stay and watch Mrglik, crossed his legs too, and in the security room in the basement of the building, the spy watching Ttfrumpt on the security cam, who also had to keep watching, crossed his legs, and so, with crossed pair of legs after crossed pair of legs, and pee suspended in a chain of bladders like the stained and tainted clouds that hovered above the city, another quiet night fell in imperial Dover.

29

When Mrglik ran past, Delaware's Stare-Eyes
#4, startled, fired into the dark room—at just
the same time that Katie yelped, hurled the lamp,
and struck his hand. The shots went wild—the
window blew out—and Jasper threw off the
bedclothes to do vengeance in his nightgown.

#4 raised his gun to fire again, his comic eye-
brows twitching.

Jasper threw himself through the air and
grabbed the boy's wrists, wrestling for the pis-
tol. #4 dragged the muzzle toward Jasper's head;
Jasper shoved the muzzle away. Wincing, the
Boy Technonaut strained at #4's grip on the gun.
The two stumbled back into the hall.

Katie and Lily rushed to Jasper's side. #4's

hand was loosening. Lily tugged at the gun—and it went off again. The bullet buried itself in the plaster of the wall.

With a cry of success, Jasper wrested the pistol free.

Now #4 was on the defensive, surrounded by three enemies, one of them armed. He scampered down the hallway.

Jasper ordered, "Halt! HALT!"

But to no avail. #4 knew Jasper, ever a gentleman, would not shoot at him—and he darted up a staircase toward the roof.

Jasper, grimacing, gave chase. The door at the top of the stairs was just sliding to a comfortable pneumatic close when the Boy Technonaut hurled it open and, back to the wall, gun close to his chest, stepped out onto the roof.

The roof deck was dark. The plastic chairs were tipped up against their tables for the night. The umbrellas were furled.

There! Jasper spied the boy in the tracksuit leaping from the parapet onto the next roof.

Jasper followed and leaped after him. #4 sprinted past coiled tubing and pigeon roosts. They ran a crazy race, zigzagging past air shafts and blimp moorings. #4 had a strong lead and made good use of it. He swerved and ducked, and finally Jasper lost track of him.

The Boy Technonaut paused, glancing around wildly. City sounds filled the night: the honking of horns, the cries of street vendors. Blue diesel fumes shouldered their way up from below, gentle and watchful as hunched crones. Jasper stepped first one way, then another, peering through the greasy smoke.

Then he spied #4. The boy was on the next roof, cupped in a vaultapult, about to be launched by an attendant into who-knew-where.

Jasper darted toward them, hoping to stop the attendant from firing.

Jasper leaped from the one roof to the other just as #4 was fired in the other direction. They passed in midair, arms spinning. The stem of the vaultapult was still *wocka-wocka-wocka* when Jasper landed.

"I want to follow that boy!" Jasper demanded to the attendant. "Make speed!"

"Fifteen cents for trip," said the attendant.

Jasper spluttered and looked down at his nightgown.

He slapped theatrically at his hips, where there were no pockets. "Can I pay you later?" he asked.

"Sorry, sir."

"Saturn's rings, man! Please?"

"This is impossible, sir. Fifteen cents."

"I beg of you."

"Eh, sir. Old saying: No dough, no throw."

Jasper scowled. "While I usually deplore this sort of tactic," he said, "I would like to point out that I am the one with the gun."

The attendant thought this over. Finally, he nodded. "You pay tomorrow?"

"I pay tomorrow. Send me where that boy went."

"Step in, sir."

Jasper clambered into the bowl of the vaulta-pult. The attendant cranked back the arm. Jasper had only done this a couple of times before, and that was during the day. Now he felt a tingly hysteria. A roller-coaster terror. Height was all around him. He was curled up, about to be thrown through the air over chasmlike streets and concrete walls. He held his breath. He jolted backward by degrees. He held on to his legs and tried to remember not to tense. He took three deep breaths and told himself that soon, he would—

WHAM! He'd been hucked.

Lights—impossible lights—moving impos-sibly quickly. He blinked rapidly. The city was spread beneath him—the domes lit by search-lights—the candles in homes—the torches carried in procession—the hotel signs half lit and half broken.

Jasper spread his arms and legs, his night-gown flapping. He could fly. *He could fly!*

Not too long until touchdown. He saw #4 ahead of him—already clambering down from the receiving trampoline and disappearing into a door.

Jasper clicked the safety-catch into place on the gun—steeled himself—relaxed his arms—and with an unbearable jolt hit the mat. He bounced.

Up into the night air again he soared. And down.

And up. And down. And up. And down.

His foe was getting away.

And up. And down. And up. And down.

His foe was probably several floors below him.

184

And up. And down. And up. And down.

And so Jasper bounced helplessly as his
enemy escaped.

30

The bouncing slowed. Jasper grabbed at the edge of the trampoline. It slipped from his grasp. Next bounce, he grabbed again. Held.

His knees still jolted, but he was steady. He clambered off the trampoline and rushed to the door.

It was an apartment building. Many of the stairs were still in place. He galloped down them, jumping over the spots where the concrete had crumbled to sand. From a landing, wide-eyed toddlers watched him pass.

Down five flights he ran and leaped. Now he could hear a jabber of voices: angry tenants who'd been shoved by #4 as he passed. They were in a crowd, on the second floor.

Jasper pushed through them and rushed to the window.

#4 was already across the street, running up a flight of stairs that led to the top of one of the ancient city walls.

By the time Jasper reached the top of those walls, #4 would be gone. The traffic in the road below was at once clogged and dangerous: mules, motorcycles, Vespas, trucks, all braying and honking and beeping and swerving around one another and shoving and shouting.

No way he could reach the boy in time. Unless—

A ladder salesman in the middle of the street, his wares strapped to his head, suddenly turned to see if it was safe to cross.

Jasper jumped from the window. He landed on the man's ladder, pranced from rung to rung across the street.

Just as he was about to leap off the ladder onto the old brick staircase opposite, the man swiveled his head to look the other way. Jasper cursed ("Crom's teeth!") and watched helplessly as he swung back out over the road. He grabbed at the stiles of the ladder to stabilize himself.

#4 had stopped ascending. He grinned down at Jasper with wolfy teeth.

Jasper looked—and saw a truck was coming. He would be knocked down into the street and flattened. The truck honked a desperate warning.

Jasper did the only thing he could. He fired the gun into the air.

The ladder salesman looked up in surprise.

And Jasper slid down the tilted ladder, arms spread like a surfer's, and hopped off onto the staircase.

The chase was on again.

#4 was on top of the wall now, scrambling past crenelations and moldering turrets with pagoda roofs.

Jasper gained the roof. He was feeling triumphant already. His opponent had lost valuable time in wolfy jeering. There was a lesson to be learned there, Jasper thought soberly as he grabbed at the boy's tracksuit.

He spun #4 around. #4 struggled.

Jasper held the boy's arms.

#4 stared at him.

Jasper stared back.

The two stood without moving.

#4's comic eyebrows wriggled.

Jasper did not budge.

#4's eyes turned to serpent slits.

Jasper glared back.

A battle of wills was going on without words or motion. The two boys trembled.

Jasper could feel his brow prickling, sweat along his neck. He shut these things out and thought only about the eyes. He concentrated all of his might upon his enemy.

He could feel #4 bending, giving in. #4's eyes snapped to human.

Through grit teeth, Jasper demanded, "Who . . . are . . . you?"

"Li'l . . . Weasel Chops . . . O'Reilly."

"Where . . . is . . . your . . . team?"

"The Royal Grant . . . Hotel."

"Who . . . are . . . they?"

"We . . . we work for . . . Bobby . . . Spandrel."

"Bobby Spandrel! My archenemy!" Jasper gasped beneath his breath. He asked, "You mean a treacherous fellow with a round, silver head?"

#4 shivered with horror. He gibbered, "Bobby . . . Spandrel . . ."

"And your Coach? And Team Mom?"

"Coach . . . and Team Mom . . . just supervise . . . the selling . . . of the artifacts."

"Where is Bobby Spandrel?"

#4's breathing was squealy and ragged. His shoulders rolled up and down. With labor, he finally said: "Vbngoom."

At that, he collapsed. Jasper watched the pupils contract from human to snake and then to asterisk. Then #4 fell to the ground, senseless.

The interrogation was over.

31

After Jasper had called an ambulance and had seen that the comatose Delaware Stare-Eyes player was well-cared for at the hospital, he called Katie and Lily at the hotel and told them that the game was afoot, and what the score was.

He met them at the Royal Grant Hotel. They were already sitting there in the lobby, looking anxious, when he strode in. "Right-o," he said. "To work!"

"Jasper?" said Katie. "First of all, how do you expect us to face seven Stare-Eyes players, their coach, and their team mom? Second of all, Mr. Genius, would you stop and look down?"

"Huhn?" said Jasper unintelligibly, and looked down. He looked up. "Aha," he said. "In my haste to ensure that my opponent's medical condition is stable, I have completely forgotten that I am not wearing clothes."

His nightgown was bedraggled. His bare feet were coated in mud.

"We already asked about the Stare-Eyes team," said Lily. "They left about an hour ago. They told the guy at the desk that they had gotten an urgent message and they couldn't stay."

"Drat," said Jasper. He thought for a minute. "About an hour ago . . . Hmm . . . Why, that's just when I was confronting Number Four on the city wall. I wouldn't be surprised if he sent them a mental message, through ESP, telling them that I had captured him. And I wouldn't be surprised if they're the ones who knocked him out—so I wouldn't discover more about their diabolical schemes!"

"That makes sense," said Lily.

"Did they leave anything in the room? Any clue or neglectful spoor?"

"Sure," said Katie. "They left a sign saying, 'We went thataway.'"

"Eureka! Which way did it point?"

"Well, when the hotel clerk took it out of the garbage and gave it to me, it pointed over there, but now it's folded up in my pocket, so it's pointed—"

"The staff disturbed the crime scene?" sputtered Jasper. "That note could have—"

"She's joking, Jasper," Lily whispered.

"Sarcasm," said Katie.

He frowned. A little stung, he said, "I guess some of us have time for larks because they are not being hurled through the air in high-speed chases."

Katie said, "And some of us have time to put on clothes before spending a night out on the town."

"Well, some of us—"

"Hey," said Lily, "let's go back to bed. We have to be up in four and a half hours to meet our guide. Let's not fight."

They stepped outside the hotel and flagged down a three-wheeled taxi. They got in, and it drove them through the skinny, steep streets, past old crumbling Baroque facades and shuttered windows, past brass shrines black with old smoke and murky pools where laundry hung to dry.

"I cannot believe that Bobby Spandrel has taken over Vbngoom," said Jasper desolately. "It was an island of peace in a world of confusion. And now—probably to get back at me—he is there stealing its treasures and beating the stuffing out of its monks."

Lily rubbed Jasper's arm awkwardly but kindly. She said, "We're going to stop him."

"It's my fault," said Jasper. "We have to get there as fast as possible. I'm the one Bobby Spandrel wants."

"What is it he wants you for?" asked Katie.

"I suspect, to get revenge for foiling all his plans."

"Like in *Jasper Dash and the Cowpoke Caper*," said Lily.

"Exactly. Most recently, he sent out thousands of fake electronic mails to people telling them they had won millions of dollars in a global lottery.

They just had to send him their bank account information, and he would give them their prize. But really, he planned to use that information to withdraw all their money and leave them penniless. But his efforts came to nothing. No one fell for the scam because Bobby Spandrel's gangster typists were such atrocious spellers."

"What does spelling have to do with it?" Katie asked.

Jasper explained, "A small error, but important. No one would freely give their bank account number to something called 'The World-Wide Lootery.' I was tipped off, and I traced Spandrel to his secret base beneath an old abandoned pulled-pork restaurant in North Carolina. I went in and busted his computers and found the priceless black diamond, the Eye of the Jaguar, and returned it to its rightful owner."

"What Eye of the Jag—"

"It must be Bobby Spandrel's World-Wide Lootery that is up at the monastery now. Don't you see, chums? Time after time, when he's been about to kill thousands or steal millions, I have stumbled upon him and tried to stop him. So, why, I think this is his revenge. He wants to lure me back to the place that means the most to me of anywhere in the world. He wants to ruin it. He wants me to suffer as he has suffered. He probably sent those artifacts you saw, Katie—the dagger, the idol, and the model of Vbngoom—to Pelt specifically so I would see them in our museum and know something was wrong in the mountains of Delaware." Heavily Jasper finished, "Those monks are probably suffering because of me." He put his hands around his own throat and stared, horrified, into the night.

The cab dropped them off in front of the wreckage of the Sky Suite.

They went in, trudged up the stairs, and got back into bed.

Lily lay in the darkness and listened to Jasper breathing in the next bunk. She could tell he was still awake. She wished there was something she could say to soothe him. She was glad they were setting out on their trek the next day. He would not be satisfied until they confronted his archenemy.

Lily wondered if she had an archenemy. She didn't think she did. She went through the possibilities in her head. She was getting sleepy.

Outside, taxis rattled through the pitted streets. Trios of drunks sang rounds in the doorways of nightclubs, their neckties loose, their shirts soaked with sweat from dancing.

Tomorrow, Lily thought to herself. *Just a few hours. Tomorrow.*

Across the dark alley, on the gargoyles, pigeons shrugged their shoulders.

PART THREE

BEYOND HIGH SMYRNA

32

Dover does not sleep at dawn. The sleep of that city is fitful; and though it is still dark at six, the people who live in those ancient streets and squares are already going about their early-morning chores. The women wash clothes in cracked fountains that once celebrated the triumphs of some long-forgotten duke; men light fires in the hearth. Boys and girls scrub their infant sisters in cauldrons, and mules sigh in their stalls. Priests trudge up stone steps to the tops of towers to chant prayers to their gods.

Three figures stood by the piled ruins of the Sky Suite and the wall of the Dupontville Fine Excellent View Stay Hotel. The mist was thick around them. Already, women walked along the

street with baskets of fried rolls on their heads, calling out prices. A man with a bicycle basket full of fresh beets rolled past, hawking his veggies.

Out of the darkness and mist came Bntno, already smiling. "Excellent children," he said. "You are ready?"

"Top o' the morning, Bntno," said Jasper, who was always chipper at dawn. "We've just been digging out our backpacks and supplies."

Lily said hello, but Katie just looked around and said, "Hi. Where's your jeep?"

"Oh, jeep," said Bntno. "We walk short way to my jeep. I leave it short way down this street."

"We're off then, chaps," said Jasper, heaving his pack up onto his back.

They followed Bntno down the street.

Now the mist was rising. Lily could see down the dark alleys. Corn hung to dry on the roofs and eaves of houses. Electrical wires were strung from old, elaborately carved windows,

windows wound around with wooden dragons, with stags and pigs, with angels and devils. Lily glanced into courtyards as they passed and saw the children coming out of tiny doors in their school uniforms: tunics and smiley-face masks of white rice paper. In one courtyard, a mangy, flea-ridden griffon lay couchant, chained to the wall, flies buzzing around its slow-blinking head. It lapped water out of an old orange juice container.

"What do these posters say?" Jasper asked their guide, pointing to the walls.

"It say . . . It say . . . 'Citizens! Your Adorable Autarch loves you! Cuddle his image like a puppy!'"

"The Autarch," muttered Jasper, "steals from the poor to give to the rich."

"That's awful," said Lily.

"If the children will please not criticize our kind and generous Autarch," said Bntno, smiling, "then maybe we will not spend the rest of the year upside down in a charcoal pit."

"Speaking of the rest of the year," said Katie, "just how far away did you park your jeep?"

"A little farther," he said. "You follow me."

Women watched the four of them from rickety porches high up on the houses.

An hour passed. Now people were done with their washing and their breakfast, and they were biking to jobs or being flung to work.

Lily looked in amazement at the high tile roofs slumped with age and growing with grass, at the goats grazing there, at the intricately decorated courtyards she spotted through arches, signs of greater days.

A wizard hanging bundles of herbs out to dry on racks watched them pass.

"Um," said Katie, a little more impatiently. "As in: Um?"

"No problems!" said Bntno merrily. "This way, inquisitive youngster!"

Another hour or two passed. Now it was full day, and the four walked through the city's great marketplace, where girls in shrouds shouted prices through megaphones, and fathers pawed through stacks of rayon socks for their children, and the delicious smells of deep-fry came from barrels over fires, and goose-boys bartered with kitchen girls. Earth-moving equipment ground and stumbled along over the potholes and cobblestones. Donkeys wandered past watermelon stands. Platoons of tusked, six-armed guardsmen from high Lumbrook in barbed helmets passed each other and slapped each other high fifteens.

Lily was mesmerized by the jumble of activity. She couldn't believe all of the color and light and sound. It was too much to take in at once. One moment, she was delighted to see children playing in the square; the next moment, she was outraged that the Autarch kept everyone so poor and so frightened. She gaped at the clatter and action and stepped carefully over the piles of ox dung.

"Hey," said Katie, "I know I might sound kind of like a . . . you know, repeating thing, but

haven't we been walking for kind of a long—"

"Just down this road, asking friend," said Bntno, putting his hands over his eyes in a gesture of respect, and running into a roadside shrine.

Two real eyes blinking behind the eyes of a crocodile idol watched them pass.

An hour and fifteen minutes later, it was getting hot and the mist had burned away entirely, leaving a deep blue sky above the glittering pagoda roofs and complicated domes and spires of the gilded temples far behind the children. The three kids and their guide were no longer in the city. The pterodactyls had come out and circled around those distant towers, crying. Bntno and his charges were on a broad road with mud-and-tin shacks on either side of it, advertising tires or handmade dentistry. Behind the shacks were cornfields and a few sick oxen tied to trees.

"Okay," said Katie. "It's ten-thirty and we've been walking since—"

"Yes, yes. There my jeep. I leave it right here." He guided them to the right, between a couple of thatched cottages, and pointed to where his jeep lay upside down in a ditch.

The three stared at the wreck.

"We turn it over before we get in," said Bntno.

"Well," said Katie, "at least we're here."

"Atoms to gluons!" Jasper exclaimed, smacking himself in the forehead. "We have to go back! I forgot to pay the vaultapult attendant his fifteen cents!"

Lily said, "I think maybe you can pay him another time."

"I'm a man of my word, Lily."

"Jasper," said Katie, with warning in her voice. "Jaaaaasper!"

"Does a man's sworn oath mean nothing? Are words mere puffs of air?"

Bntno was attaching ropes to the side of the jeep. "Not to go back now, child. We pull jeep up."

A large group of locals had come out of their businesses to watch Bntno struggle with his jeep. Now they all lent a hand with the ropes. Katie, Lily, and Jasper also yanked. In no time whatsoever, the jeep had flipped back over. It was not in great shape. There was a line of dirt and silt wavering across its windshield where the water had lapped for some days.

And once they got in and started driving, they realized there was probably some kind of problem with the rear axle, because they wobbled. And there were soft-shell crabs on the seats.

They tossed the crabs and headed toward the forests of the north.

33

I am afraid that now comes the part in the novel of foreign adventure that I really can't stand. We have a lull in the action, so the characters get informative about local industries: weaving, pottery, major imports and exports, farming techniques, etc. They have idiotic conversations like "Now, how do the interesting people in this country make these colorful baskets?" or "So, what about smelting?"

They talk about the life cycle and running speed of some animal they drive past or about the unusual customs they see. The whole time, you just want the story to get back to all the chasing and the riddles and the cabin in the woods and the fighting, but no, all you get are three pages on the history of origami. It's like seeing someone's vacation slides but in a room half filled with cold water and a stingray.*

For several hours, they had driven through rice fields. Dover had dwindled to a speck on the horizon. They had passed through small towns, half-timbered houses built over irrigation ditches. Jasper had asked many intense questions about local vegetable farming and, later, about the pasta fields that waved in the welcome breezes beneath the hot sun. They stopped to pluck some ziti for lunch.

The last large town they passed in the plains was Smyrna, built upon a great peak of stone, a massive granite boulder that jutted up out of the grasslands, houses clinging to its sides. At its highest point stood the ruined fortress where, four centuries before, the last few men and women of Smyrna had withstood the ferocious attack of the Silent Butchers of Deakyneville.

By three o'clock, they had reached the

---

*Yes, it happened to me. Thank you, Burgess Lipton Jr., for a lovely evening. Next time you go to the Dakotas with your digital camera, please stay there.

foothills of the mountains. Forest grew upon the slopes. The jeep bumped and rattled through little village squares where people squatted in a few shops that sold lentils and spices or copper wire.

Bntno sang the old, wailing songs of Dover. At first Lily was thrilled to hear them, but after an hour or two, she had a headache. When he wouldn't stop singing twenty or thirty verses per song, Katie tried to interrupt with questions, at first about what the words might mean ("That's so interesting. So what do the—"; "Could you translate what you—"; "Um, could you just keep your hands on the wheel? And could you—"), and then, later, just questions of any kind that might make him stop singing. ("Now, how do the interesting people of this state make these colorful baskets?"; "So, what about smelting?")

The jeep juddered over hills where red clay houses stood among rich orchards and bridges swung over deep, leafy ravines.

They stayed that night in a village. They ate

at a small tavern there, and sat outside on the porch, seeing the billion stars above them and hearing the wild dogs bark in the forest. There were lights far up in the mountains—lonely lights—lights from people who saw others only once every few months. Soon, the three friends would be up in those mountains. They would be far from any civilization, any help.

The night smelled of orchids and green.

In the morning, they left behind the last villages. They rambled down the far side of the foothills, and they were in a jungle valley. Moss grew on the trees, and the wide, waxen leaves of exotic plants hung low over the rutted dirt track. Monkeys watched the jeep from trees.

As they drove, Jasper scanned Lisa Buldene's *There and Back Again*™ for clues as to how to find the mountain monastery.

"It mentions the four mountains," Jasper reported. "Their names are Drgsl, Minndfl, Bdreth, and Tlmp. Vbngoom lies atop Tlmp."

"I thought they were supposed to have

supersecret names that no mortals knew," said Katie.

"Well," said Jasper, somewhat bothered, "I guess some mortals now know them. The mortals who have looked them up in the index."

Lily could tell that Jasper was a little hurt that his secret mountains were in the book's index. She asked him gently, "What does the book say about the mountains?"

Jostled by the road, Jasper held the book up close to his eyes and, elbows bobbing, read out: "'Though the Four Peaks look the same height, trekkers will find that Mount Minndfl is actually considerably shorter than the nearby peak covered with deceptively inviting pine woods. English explorer and adventurer Leslie Arbuckle-Smythe climbed both that forested peak—despite its imposing height—and Mount Bdreth because he was too superstitious to climb near the ancient, rune-inscribed pillar that stands on one of the other mountains.'"

"Too superstitious?" asked Lily. "What does it mean by that?"

"He was a fellow archaeologist and adventurer," said Jasper. "After a few scrapes, we think twice about anything that might get us bitten by a mummified cat."

"I mean, what was he worried about with the pillar?"

Jasper flipped a few pages. "Doesn't say," he said. "But it reminds us this is a carry-in, carry-out park."

They drove through the jungle wastes. The heavy green foliage hung all around them. Wild boar scampered out of their way. Swamps gleamed through the trees.

They saw no sign of civilization. They now saw no house, no farm, no logging teams or goatherds. No one. Birds flew above them. Monkeys called from branches. The wilderness was complete.

That night, they pulled off the track and pitched their tents in the jungle. Lily was a little scared of sleeping outside when unknown things lurked in the woods. Jasper tried to reassure her, but she was not used to jungle adventures in the way that he was, and she found herself lying awake, listening as things shuffled and slid through the underbrush.

At last, exhausted by a day of being thrown around in the jeep, she fell asleep. She had not slept long, however, when Katie shook her awake.

"Lily," whispered Katie. "There's someone coming."

Lily's heart froze in her chest. She listened.

Yes, she too could hear a jeep engine, hear the quiet crunch of gravel under tires as someone drove slowly along the road. As if someone was looking for someone.

She could see the headlights through the fabric of the tent. They lay awake and panicked. They both hoped that Jasper was silently awake, too. They both thought about what to do.

The strange jeep stopped and the engine idled. There was a swoop of light—a flashlight being played across the tents—and then it was snapped off. There was a lot of crunching and snapping as the jeep turned around. The girls lay rigid, each balanced on an elbow, afraid to move.

Then they heard the mysterious jeep head back up the road the way it had come.

"It's going," said Lily. "Thank goodness."

"Yeah, thank goodness," said Katie. "Unless those sounds just after the flashlight switched off were someone quietly getting out of the jeep."

Lily, in the pitch-black, could feel herself turning pale.

34

"Jasper," hissed Katie through the wall of her tent. "Jas!"

"I saw it," he whispered back. "I'll rev up my atomic torch. Let's take a look." With a sound like a very small UFO rounding Neptune, Jasper's light filled his tent.

Carefully they crawled outside into the black night. Bntno still lay snoring in his tent. Lily held her flashlight at the ready, but she didn't turn it on—thinking that it was better if they kept themselves at least somewhat hidden in the darkness.

The three of them stood side by side, Jasper in the middle, the valiant beams of his atomic torch sweeping the ferns and mossy trunks. Nothing moved.

Far off, monkeys howled.

Jasper gestured for the other two to walk away from his light. If there was anyone else there, they'd be blinded and wouldn't be able to see Lily and Katie.

The three moved forward and into the road. Each step was agony, announced by snaps and grindings beneath their feet. Each footfall might have well been an explosion. If anyone was crouched in the bushes, listening, he would have no trouble telling where and how many of them they were.

Lily now switched on her flashlight. She ran it over the ruts and tracks, each pebble picked out in the stark glare. "Here's where the other car turned around," she whispered.

Jasper and Katie headed over toward her. She ran her light along the treaded tire tracks.

"And here," she said in a voice strangled with horror, "is the footprint where someone got out."

35

Sunrise found the three friends huddled around the remains of a fire, looking pale, jittery, and thin. They had not slept a wink all night. They had been waiting for someone to prowl out of the darkness with a gleaming blade.

The first thing they had done was to compare the tire tracks in the dust to Jasper's memory of the white van's tire tracks, to see if maybe this was the Stare-Eyes team again, but Jasper said that no, this was a jeep about the size of their own. Then they had carefully searched the whole area for more footprints, and had found a few near Bntno's jeep. But from there the tracks led into the jungle, and soon the spongy plants hid all traces of their mysterious visitor. There was no further sign of him, and there was no telling when he might return.

So they waited through the night.

Toward dawn, an incredible chorus of birdsong and snakesong arose in the jungle around them, the macaws singing high in the branches, the vipers and pythons swaying on the ground below, emitting their weird, worshipful chirps for the sun that warmed them.

A booming voice startled the three. "Glad day, little ones!" Bntno had finally woken up and clomped out of his tent in his rubber shoes. He stretched. "Sleep, it is the glorious restorer!" he exclaimed. Then he regarded the three with new interest. "Maybe you have made eggs?"

"We have not made eggs," said Jasper sourly. "We were disturbed in the middle of the night by a strange jeep that appeared to be looking for us, which dropped off someone when it found us."

"Ah," said Bntno. "This is probably government spy." He began to take down his tent. "We leave in half an hour, okay?"

"How much farther until we reach the four mountains?" asked Jasper. "I reckoned on about three days' driving."

"Three days?!" Katie protested. "You can't *drive* straight north in Delaware for three days. You'd end up in Canada."

"Katie," whispered Lily. "I really think it's better if you let this one go."

In half an hour they had packed their tents and sleeping bags in the jeep and were ready to go. Bntno, humming Doverian pop, hopped into the driver's seat, twisted the key in the ignition, and said, "Now we is rock and roll, disco dancer!" He clapped his hands.

The engine turned over a few times and the jeep rattled about ten feet, then there was an awful noise. The jeep quit.

Bntno tried the key again. Nothing. The engine choked and died.

"One minutes, disco dancer," he said, holding up his finger. He climbed out, went in front of the jeep, and opened the hood.

Jasper got out to help look for the problem.

"This jeep has been upside down in a ditch full of rainwater," said Katie. "Do they really need to *look* for the problem?"

Jasper had an idea. He went around to the side of the jeep. He fiddled with the lid of the gas tank. He pulled it off, ran his finger along its edge, and sniffed his finger.

"Grave news," he said. "The jeep has been sabotaged. Our mysterious visitor has put sugar in our gas tank." He smelled again. "Hmm. And a refreshing hint of cinnamon and cloves. We clearly are not dealing with your average roustabout ruffian here."

There was nothing for it. They were going to have to walk.

"It's going to take *weeks* to walk," said Katie. "Do we even have enough food?"

"There is one way we can walk," said Bntno. "Shortcut. It is in a very dangerous place, Greylag—a ruined city with very many creature—but there is a bridge over the Drawyer

River there. I do not say it before, because we had jeep and jeep could not go across this bridge in Greylag, but if you want to make walk shorter, we could go on this bridge. Cut off many days."

Jasper thought about it. "Time is of the essence," he said. "It was three days ago that I received that mental message from Drgnan Pghlik. Who knows what Bobby Spandrel and his World-Wide Lootery might be up to by now at the monastery?"

"Are you sure this is a good idea?" said Lily. "It might not be worth it to go through the ruined city if there are a lot of . . . creatures."

"I have my ray gun," said Jasper confidently. "Somewhere." He began patting his backpack.

"What kind of creatures?" Katie asked Bntno.

"Oh, tooth creatures. Stompy creatures. Old creatures."

"Those don't sound like a good kind of creatures," Katie said to Jasper.

Jasper looked down. "You're right," he said. "I can't ask you to risk your lives for my friend. But I must go that way. I must take the shortest route possible to reach Vbngoom. Give me those two packs, and I will set off."

Katie and Lily exchanged a look.

"If you go that way, Jasper, we're all going that way," said Katie. "We're not going to let you do something that dangerous alone."

"Yeah," said Lily. "We're with you, whatever happens."

"Here. I'll even take your extra pack," said Katie, grappling it onto her shoulder.

"You don't need to take my extra pack," said Jasper.

"We stick together," said Katie.

Jasper was clearly moved. "By the squealing fruits of Arcturus, you are the best friends a man could have," he said.

They pulled their other packs out of the jeep and prepared the long walk toward the terrors of the jungle.

36

They tromped along the white, chalky road
through the rain forest. Hours had gone by.

The sun was swelteringly hot. Lily felt like all of
her bones were made of warm lead. She was sweating so much it was embarrassing. She couldn't walk
as fast or as far as Jasper or Katie. She kept taking swigs from her canteen, but she was afraid she
would run out of water if she wasn't careful.

Bntno sang Doverian pop tunes, playing air
guitar.

"Just think," said Katie. "We would have
been driving this whole way and it would have
taken us about twenty-five minutes to get this
far if it hadn't been for that jerk last night and
his sugar. When I get my hands on him . . ." She

shifted the weight of the extra bag on her shoulder. It rattled and clanked. "What's in here, anyway?" she asked Jasper.

"Supplies," he answered vaguely. "You know. Supplies."

"What supplies?" Katie asked. "It weighs like a million tons."

Lily, who had not spoken for a while, suddenly said, "The government must have heard enough of our plans through the clown picture in the hotel room to know where we're going. Maybe they sent someone to trail us. But if they want to find out where Vbngoom is, why would they sabotage our jeep and stop us from getting there?"

"Hmm," Jasper mused. "That is an excellent question."

"But they're probably still out here," said Katie. "You saw the footprints."

After this discussion, the three of them had the creeping feeling that someone was following them. Every once in a while, one of them would stop and wheel around—but there was nothing behind them but the white road, the green leaves, and the blue sky. They walked and they sweated.

Late that afternoon they came to a huge stone post, green with moss, out of which peered toothy gargoyle faces and long words in some forgotten script. "This is the place," said Bntno. "Here we take path."

They were just starting down the path when they heard a distant sound. The sound of an engine.

None of them thought, *We're saved!* They knew exactly what it would be before it even reached them.

"Hide!" said Jasper, but Lily and Katie had already barreled down the path and were peering back toward the road out of the ferns. Bntno, confused, followed them.

The white van. It rolled along the track. All of the players within stared straight ahead. Team Mom drove, holding her cigarette out the window.

The van passed the place where the stone post marked the point where the path diverged from the road. It continued down the road, throwing up clouds of white dust behind it.

"Those dastards," said Jasper. He turned to Bntno. "Is there any way we can reach Vbngoom by foot before them?"

"No," said Bntno. "This way is shorter, but still long time by feets."

"Still," said Jasper, "we've got to try."

And with renewed vigor, the four of them set off along the path toward Greylag, the ruined city, haunt of stompy creatures, and the treacherous bridge over the mighty river Drawyer.

37

Shortly before nightfall, they came upon an abandoned government army base by the path. The walls were of green metal, scratched and dented. The windows were busted. By the side of the building, there was an old, crumpled radio tower on a base of moss-covered concrete.

Though it was creepy, they decided to stay there overnight. They went inside. All of the furniture was broken, and there were leaves on the floor.

Bntno explained that, not to worry, it was probably a base where the army had conducted research on the dinosaurs of the hills, or had blocked the approach of the lizard people of Odessa Heights.

Suddenly, Lily didn't have a very good feeling.

They spread out their sleeping bags. Jasper and Lily went out to collect firewood while Katie stayed inside, struggling with the soft-drink machine, whacking the broad plastic buttons and loudly demanding the final few rusting cans of Dr Pepper.

They lit a fire outside. They ate lentil stew and black bread. Insects sang all around them.

Lily was frightened of the dark that night. She was embarrassed, but she couldn't help looking into the shadows and seeing strange shapes. "By dinosaurs," said Lily, "do you mean big lizards?"

"Dinosaurs," Bntno said. "Yes? Tyranno-saurus. Ankylosaurus. Stegosaurus."

"Not extinct?" Lily asked.

"Not in Delaware. Live still in Delaware."

"Great," said Katie, chewing irritably. "Dinosaurs. Surviving here. Just had to, didn't they?" She protested grumpily, "It's ridiculous.

The tyrannosaurus and stegosaurus don't even come from the same, like, *period*. The tyrannosaurus is from the Cretaceous period and the stegosaurus is the Jurassic or something."

Jasper was clearly impressed. "Katie," he said, "I didn't realize you knew so much about dinosaurs."

"Yeah," said Katie resentfully. "I had to redo a class project on them when I was in fifth grade. They asked us to make a model of a dinosaur, so I made one by covering one of my old Star-Wonder Glitter-Ponies with clay. You know, I gave him wings and stuff. The teacher didn't like it because he said there wasn't a real dinosaur that had wings and four legs. And a pink-and-blue sparkly mane. He gave me a D minus and said it was a sad day for paleontology."

"I'm worried about the dinosaurs," Lily said.

"Oh," said Bntno, smiling broadly, "do not fear dinosaurs tonight. They do not come here. Not a thing where you should be afraid of."

Bntno squinted up into the foothills. "Lively children," he said, "will you turn your eyes toward those lights?"

They looked where he pointed. Far, far away—several miles—there were lights in the hills.

"Now there, you be afraid. See? Fires," said Bntno. "The Kangaroo-Riders of Armstrong. Cannibals. Very bad. Very bad peoples."

"Cannibals?" said Katie.

"If they catches you, excellent girl, yes, you are cooked in tinfoils, with tomato and cilantro."

"Dastards," Jasper whispered. "I cannot stand cilantro."

Lily was eager to change the subject. Luckily, Katie said, "Hey, Jas, is there anything to drink in your extra backpack here?"

Lily asked her, "Didn't you, um, have any luck with the drink machine?"

Grim-faced, Katie held out two old, grimy bottles of Tyrant Splash. "So do you have anything else to drink?" she asked. "I'm getting thirsty. I heart carbonation."

"In the backpack?" said Jasper. "No. Nothing."

"It's heavy," said Katie.

Jasper was flustered. "Katie, I'm terribly sorry I let you carry it. It's my extra bag and I should—"

"That's fine, Jas," said Katie, shrugging.

"No!" said Bntno suddenly. "No, thirsty girl. Me. I will carry it tomorrow. In the excellent Old World charm of Delaware, we say, the little lady should never be carry the heavy bag. In our excellent Old World charm, we say the little lady, she should just bake corn, lie hammock, paint her eyebrow—"

"Thanks for the offer. But first, I'm not a 'little lady.' And second, I have more than one eyebrow. And third—"

"No, no, defiant youngster," Bntno insisted. "I will carry this other bag."

"I *love* carrying the extra bag," said Katie.

"But I happen to be tired and thirsty, that's all."

"Perhaps," said Jasper shyly, "you would like some Gargletine Instant Breakfast Drink?"

Katie fixed him with a long, level stare. Gargletine™ caused hysteria in lab rats and took the brown off horses. "Maybe not," said Katie. "But thanks."

"Okay," said Bntno, "if the little girl does not want me to carry the bag . . ."

Katie was in no mood to be called a "little girl." She was about to stand up to her full height and give him a piece of her mind when, off in the jungle, they heard a distant roar, some miles away, like a monstrous promise for tomorrow.

They stopped talking. The roaring in the distance faded.

They looked nervously at each other. They suddenly didn't have much to say. After that, they all soon went to bed.

That night, none of the three kids could sleep. Bntno kept muttering in his dreams. Every time one of them almost dropped off, they thought they heard something outside the compound. Things moved through the shrubberies.

It was only as dawn came that they fell asleep, Jasper with his ray gun cradled by his cheek.

At nine, they got up and packed their sleeping bags. Katie was still determined to get something fizzy to drink out of the old vending machine. Lily got the feeling that Katie's anger at the machine was somewhat personal. Katie went around and collected everyone's change and stood in front of the machine, feeding it coins, slapping its sides, and yelling at it. When Katie had run through everyone's change, she went outside where the others were waiting. They looked solemn and wary. She looked frustrated.

"Did you get anything out of the machine?" Jasper asked.

"A rodent," she said miserably. "I think it was a capybara."

"Someone was here last night," said Lily. She pointed at the ground. There were footprints from a pair of men's boots in the soft, black dirt. They circled the building. There were many of them just outside the shattered window of the room where the four travelers had slept—as if someone had crouched there a long while, shifting position carefully—listening through the night.

38

All day they marched through grove and clump. The jungle was hot, rotten. Fur grew on the trees. All four of them were sweating. Far off they could hear the grousing of the dinosaurs, the hysteria of monkeys.

They had not seen any dinosaurs yet—and Lily was happy to keep it that way.

They had seen another clue at the military base before they set out. Whoever had been sneaking around the night before had written a message on the door in fading Magic Marker. It said, in English, REMEMBER YOU . . .—and then the intruder had run out of ink. The door had no more to say.

Lily was not enjoying the trip. Her head was surrounded by a turban of flies. When she tried to brush them out of the air, or out of her hair, they gathered around her hand like a wristlet. They would not go away.

But it was more than that. She was frightened of what lived in the jungle. She knew that Katie was used to dealing with monsters, but Lily was not. On the far slopes, she could hear the distant crash of allosauruses through ferns and baobabs. She could almost hear their size. And she knew that she and her friends were headed straight for one of the most dangerous, dinosaur-infested places in all of Delaware.

"This afternoon, visitor children," said Bntno, "we come to the ruined city of Greylag. Very ancient city. Large amount of monster."

"We have my ray gun," said Jasper.

"I'm a little worried about this," said Katie.

"Yeah," said Lily hesitantly. "Do we have a plan?"

"We go through this city, yes? To bridge. We cross bridge real quick, only lose one of us by snatching."

"Great," said Katie. "How do we decide which one of us?"

Bntno laughed. "Very droll friend," he said, "monster decides!" He acted out the monster choosing. He pointed at the air. "Which for lunch? Hmm! This one tasty!"

"It's not funny," said Lily. "How are we going to get through these ruins alive?"

Bntno smiled. "Old saying of Delaware: Slow girl asks most questions about running."

Lily was embarrassed. She caught Katie casting a glance back. Lily knew that the others were thinking of her as the slow one, the one in the most danger. And they weren't wrong.

She didn't know what to say. She didn't want to seem like a coward, but out of the four of them, she was the one person with almost no experience of towering evil. Bntno had been to this city before. Katie had escaped from centipedes the size of commuter trains. Jasper had fought his share of sea-serpents, lunar ogres, carnivorous swamps, battle bots, tankopods, and Saturnian blimp-beasts with suctiony mouths, bundles of eyes, and weird whistling songs sung entirely in chlorine.

Lily, on the other hand, had only encountered some irritable whales. She saw Katie looking back at her again, concerned.

Katie offered, "Maybe Jasper should go on ahead and Lily and I can stay here on this side of the city. We'll walk back along the path to the gravel road."

Jasper thought about this and said, "Yes, that sounds like a good plan, Katie. I don't want to put either of you in danger."

Lily protested, "I don't want to slow us down."

Both of her friends rushed to say she wasn't slowing anyone down, no way, don't worry. She could tell by the way they rushed to reassure her that they didn't mean it. She really was slowing them down.

"I hope no one slow us down . . . ," said Bntno, holding his finger up in the air.

"No one is slowing us down, Bntno," said Jasper firmly.

". . . because listen."

They listened. They heard a distant shrieking.

"What is it?" muttered Jasper. "Dinosaurs?"

"Triceratops?" whispered Katie. ". . . es?"

Dramatically Bntno declared, "I think, the Kangaroo-Riders of Armstrong. They are move to here."

"Huh?" said Katie.

Bntno remained silent, still holding his finger up. The rest fell silent, too.

Then they heard the drums in the forest. Then they heard the triumphant yelps. Yelps of men on the hunt. Yelps broken by *Oomph*s and *Orkkk*s as steeds hit the ground and bounced, knocking the wind out of their riders. The four heard the cannibals hopping through the wood— and they heard them getting closer.

39

"Einstein's ghost!" exclaimed Jasper. "We'd better make ourselves scarce!"

Bntno was already rushing down the path, his hands spread, slapping at leaves as he went. The other three followed, their backpacks rattling. They scrambled through the wood.

Lily saw that Katie was keeping an eye on her, running at Lily's speed so Lily wouldn't fall behind.

The hunt drums sputtered distantly through the palms like something caught in the blades of a fan. *Buttabuttabuttabuttabutta.* The high, arched war cries drew closer, angry and jolted.

"You . . . don't need to . . . run slower. . . because of me," Lily said to Katie.

"I'm not," said Katie. "I'm enjoying the scenery." She leaped over a fallen trunk. "Great vacation. Thanks, Jasper, wherever you are."

They were barreling down a slope now, into a valley. Bntno was in the lead. Jasper had stopped and, ray gun held aloft, stood by the path, waiting for Katie and Lily to pass.

Just as they were by his side, he barked, "They're here!" And for a nice, comfortable moment the girls thought he meant the two of them.

But he did not.

Lily turned her head back and looked.

The cannibals of Delaware sifted suddenly out of the trees—they battered down through the wood, spears and tridents raised, kangaroos darting over branch and hummock, slamming to earth, leaping.

Bntno was so far ahead he could barely be seen. Lily ran after him as fast as she had ever run, her scratched arms flailing, her heart thumping as loud as her feet, her mouth open, hearing the wreckage of leaf and tree behind her.

Soon Bntno was out of sight. Lily had only the path to guide her, and she stumbled along it beside Katie, terrified. Then she looked up.

A chieftain stood blocking the path in front of her, arms crossed.

Jasper, Katie, and Lily had stopped running. They were already surrounded.

Kangaroos and their riders were everywhere.

With cruel shrieks and hooting calls, the cannibals of Delaware dismounted and began to pace toward the three friends. Except for six

who, disoriented by all the hopping, paced in the wrong direction, spun in circles, or went to throw up in the bushes. The rest, however, looked menacing. They looked hungry. They dressed in loincloths and terrycloth sweatbands. They were greased, and their hair was long and shaggy like rockers'. In their hands were spears, long forks, chips and salsa, and, cradled in one man's arms, a Cobb salad in Saran Wrap.

Their kangaroos hunkered behind them, waiting for the slaughter.

The chief stood on the path right in front of Lily, Jasper, and Katie. He wore a headdress— a busy, brutal confection of pheasant wings, rat skulls, and sequins—and an old barbecue apron that said I'M HERE WITH SCRUMPTIOUS →.

He smiled grimly at the three friends. He laughed. He called orders to his warriors in his unknown language.

Lily felt weak. Her arms dropped to her sides. There was nowhere to run.

40

Lily looked from scowl to frown to spiteful grin. She sought mercy. The faces offered nothing but a smorgasbord of hate with a dessert-cart of sweet murder.

And Lily and her friends were on that menu.

It was at this point that some late riders arrived, thumping through the wood.

As they whalloped up and yanked on their reins, they called something down to their chief. Whatever it was, it took a long time to say. It appeared they were having an argument. Several of them pointed at one another and jabbered. Their chief responded with anger.

Katie, Jasper, and Lily exchanged glances. They did not understand what the argument was about, but they had a feeling that any disagreement might be used to their advantage.

The chief was yelling and waving his hands around. The warriors bickered, and he replied sharply, shaking his snake-headed staff, bellowing in their harsh, ancient language that rang with the sounds of metal, battle, and clash—a tongue calling to mind the barbarians of the steppes, the night fires in the jungle, cruel raiders in dragon-prowed ships, the sack of cities, and the death of forest-kings.*

While they were occupied arguing, Jasper carefully raised his ray gun.

The chief kept yelling.

So Jasper fired near the man's feet.

The chieftain yelped and looked down. Where the beam had pierced, the leaves burned. The chieftain jumped back.

Jasper grabbed Lily's wrist and ran past the

---

*Translation: "Another potato salad??!? I thought Yrrgta signed up to bring the potato salad! What are we going to do with three bowls of stinkin' potato salad? And did any of you brain trusts think about soda pop?"

man—and Katie followed. They bolted down the path. The cannibals watched them, astounded.

Jasper turned and fired a few more laser bolts back into the trees. Shouts and exclamations of anger reached them. Cannibals grabbed at their spears and scrambled for their war-joeys.

Leaping over logs, skidding down slopes, spattering brooks, the three kids fled. Soon they could hear the pounding of kangaroos behind them.

Jasper stopped his flight and stood astraddle the path, gun raised in both hands, one eye a-squint. Needles of blue flame beat through the trees. For a moment, the warriors halted, their steeds rearing back on nervous, tawny legs. Jasper waved his gun and yelled, "There's more where that came from, you rascals!" Again, he pulled the trigger.

The trigger clicked. No fire.

He added, ". . . as soon as I dig in my rucksack for some triple-A batteries."

And began to run again.

The whole messy, bouncy cavalcade poured on down the hillside after him.

"We're . . . never . . . going to make it . . . ," said Katie. She kept grabbing at Lily's hand, yanking her friend. Lily stumbled—desperate for speed—reaching out for her faster pal.

Jasper screamed, "They're coming!"

"Do you think . . . ," said Katie, "they'll marinate us first? Because I really wrinkle in vinegar."

Lily didn't answer.

Then it was over, it seemed. Scowling kangaroos were on either side of them. Men waved forks.

Lily's heart broke. She could run no more.

"I give up," said Katie, also slowing. "All I'm doing is toughening my flank steaks."

"We can get out of this, chums," said Jasper. "I will not die without dignity. And a complete list of the sides I shall be served with."

But as they stopped and turned to meet their baker, they realized that their pursuers were silent. All over the slope, the warriors hunched atop their twitch-nosed steeds. They did not move.

They stared in horror.

Jasper, Lily, and Katie looked up.

They had just passed under a stone arch. They looked down the path, the way they had been running.

There were buildings. Stone buildings. And a giant, flame-eyed statue of a skeleton.

Suddenly, the three realized that the cannibals would not be capturing them. The cannibals were afraid. The cannibals pointed at the city and muttered words in their language.

The cannibals turned silently and fled.

They leaped back up the slope, hardly daring to look behind them. The chief touched himself on the forehead in a blessing and whispered a prayer. Then he ran.

Soon, all that was left were several spears discarded in the rush and a pile of s'more fixins.

And so our three heroes found themselves in the ruined, monster-haunted city of Greylag.

41

No one knows who built Greylag; none can say if they were of the race of men or some older, forgotten race that walked upon the earth when the brachiosaurus still made his home in the swamps and the allosaur still gazed out from the hills at dusk, razor teeth glinting in the sunset, and called her hideous children home.

Lily, Katie, and Jasper walked down a flight of steps inhumanly large and found themselves in a ruined square. The statue of the skeleton kept watch, much of his legs chipped off when the temple by which he had stood had been smashed some hundreds of years before.

Vines hung all around them. They gazed up and saw a green sky full of bright birds.

A whisper of a shoe on sand—they jumped—

and saw Bntno seated on a fallen pillar, eating a roast beef sandwich with horseradish.

"Hello, little guests!" he said, smiling.

"Ah," said Jasper, a little nettled. "Bntno."

"You all is looking well—but not well-done. Still rare. Ha? Yes? This just being a joke. This just being a thing I say." He laughed and took a bite of his sandwich.

"You cleared out pretty quickly," said Katie. "When the going got tough."

"Oh, indeed. I am the very fast runner."

"You set a record," said Katie. "You beat us all."

"I fold up sandwich, and we walk through city. Now very quiet. Very quiet. Shush, shush! This is, generally, place of doom." He wrapped up the sandwich in a piece of tinfoil, running his tongue around his teeth. He stuck the sandwich back in his backpack. He gestured, and they followed him into the ruined city of monsters.

The stones of that place were massive. It was built of granite, yes, but also of black basalt and slabs of crystal. Its towers were in ruin; most of the walls were fallen, and upon them grew the banyan tree and vine. Wild orchids bobbed in the ancient alleyways. Huge faces were cracked apart by roots.

Bntno walked, keeping his body low, stepping carefully to avoid scraping his rubber soles along the gritty flagstones. The others followed his lead. They paused before each ancient avenue to make sure that nothing terrible scuttled along it seeking food.

"We must leave city before night," whispered Bntno at one point, shifting his eyes from side to side, spidering his fingers around. "We stay in night, then very, very bad chomping."

Lily felt like she couldn't breathe.

It didn't help that Bntno almost immediately got them lost.

Jasper pointed out, "We've passed that statue seven times in the last hour."

"Very popular," said Bntno. "Who don't like that statue?"

"We're going in circles," said Jasper.

"Not circles," said Bntno. "Irregular polygons."

"Oh, come on!" complained Katie.

"No," said Jasper ruefully, "he's right. Maybe a trapezoid."

They wandered through squares and past palaces. Temples lay slumped over in the streets. They passed courtyards and brackish pools.

Once, they saw a tiny dinosaur head on a long, serpentine neck crane itself above a pyramid. They jumped, startled, but the creature just browsed on vines.

They crept away as quickly as they could.

"It getting dark," said Bntno. He told them sadly, "I would run away now and leave my jolly friends behind if I could find quick exit."

The jungle quieted around them. Monkeys stopped howling. The weird rose of dying light fell on the ancient walls. It hung in the steamy atmosphere so the air itself looked golden and perfumed.

And then evening fell. Everything was gray and unclear. Each black entrance to a house, each pit leading to unimaginable caverns, sent little chills of panic through Lily's limbs. Danger could be anywhere.

Jasper whispered, "At least the cannibals and the monsters will stop whoever's been following us."

"Great," said Katie. "Thanks for this whole adventure. I'm really enjoying it."

They passed by a huge dome inscribed with ancient words.

Just at bloody sunset, they saw a procession of ghosts. It was on one of the main avenues. They were of a tall race dressed in robes, with faces like twisted and fingered clay. They walked sorrowfully through the city and disappeared.

Somewhere, in the ruined plazas, a bell tolled.

Bntno fell to his knees, touched his hands to his forehead in a prayer, and moaned.

"I guess this isn't good," said Katie.

"Let's keep going," said Lily, gripping her own fingers. "We have to find that bridge."

Bntno got up and started scuttling forward. The others rushed to follow him.

They no longer worried about making noise. They were too panicked, all of them. Jasper had his atomic torch in one hand and his ray gun clutched in the other. They scampered through the empty squares.

Then Bntno held out his hand—they skated to a stop.

There, in the lee of an ancient drive-thru restaurant, was the nest of some carnivorous dinosaur, lying like a snoring, saw-jawed minivan among tamped-down grasses and a clutch of huge eggs. The monster was maybe thirty feet long from its head to the tip of its tail, which was wrapped around the beast like a feather boa on a sleeping starlet. The meat-eater stirred in her sleep and gently licked her eggs.

"A Tyrannosaurus rex," gasped Jasper.

"An allosaurus," said Katie. "If we're quiet, maybe we can sneak past."

"Is it an allosaurus? It does look like a T. rex."

"Yeah. The short horns near the eyes mean it's an allosaurus."

"Perhaps you're right. But I believe it is a T. rex based on its size. It seems to me much larger than an allosaurus."

"Okay, you may have a Ph.D. in archeology or whatever. But I redid that dinosaur report. It's a—"

"Um," said Lily urgently, and they saw the monster stirred in her sleep.

They shut up and crept around the sweet-scented nest.

Maybe they would have made it if, when they had passed it, Jasper, who was in a very unfortunately strained mood, had not said, "I believe the Tyrannosaurus rex has fallen back asleep."

"Jasper," Katie protested, "look at the horned ridges by—"

"The forearms are—"

The massive head swiveled up.

They all saw it lurch in the gloom.

Lily grabbed their hands and pulled them forward.

And then, terrible to hear, came the sound of stomping.

They didn't turn to look. They didn't turn to see that massive gut, those terrible claws springing along the empty avenue—those awful, ancient features twisted in an hideous, toothy grin, because they didn't want to know that something so massive might seek their flesh, snatch them up, tear them to pieces.

They ran.

42

Through the dark, falling over one another, the light from Jasper's atomic torch wheeling across the battered walls, they fled. They felt the earth shake beneath them. Bntno let out a continual whine.

Their guide led them through the maze of streets and through the nightmare eve, where things slithered in the catacombs and chuckled in old windows. The dinosaur stomped behind them.

"Maybe if we dodged into a building, the T. rex couldn't follow us!" Jasper shouted.

"But then we'd still be followed," Katie called back, "by the *allosaurus* that's chasing us!"

"While I respect your hypothesis—"

"La la la la la! Not listening!"

"The therapod's two, rather than three fingers, on the anterior claws suggest to me—"

Katie sang brashly, *"It was an A! It was an L! It was an A. L. L.-o-saurus! That's what's about to gore us! I wish it would—"*

"T. rex!"

". . . ignore us!"

"Um, guys?" said Lily. "Maybe we should—"

They stopped arguing. The crashing footsteps were getting closer. The four ran down a wide street, jolting at each footfall of the colossus.

Suddenly, Bntno skidded in his tracks. "No!" he said. "You sing so much my brain is scramble! This way!"

Katie, Lily, and Jasper turned in horror to look at him. He was pointing back toward the dimly seen bulk of the giant dino.

"I see the door to bridge!" he said. He gestured again back the way they had come. "We pass! There!" he said, and pointed at a door.

And so they ran right toward the dinosaur.

It thundered toward them.

They turned a sharp left.

They were inside a building. Jaws snapped at the door. Huge, greasy fingers thumped after them, a two-clawed hand scuffled around in the darkened chamber. The dinosaur couldn't fit in.

"Thank goodness," said Jasper, trying to be the peacemaker, "that therapods such as the Tyranno-saurus rex . . . and the, um, allosaurus have such short, weak forearms."

Katie looked at him gratefully and nodded.

They ran down a flight of stairs.

And they were standing before a wide chasm. Its walls were covered in moss and baby tears. Luminous fungus lit it like a warm green noon. Tiger lilies grew in nooks. Deep in the chasm, too far down to see, a river rushed over rocks and boulders.

A stone bridge led across the chasm to the other side.

"Shortcut," said Bntno. "No problem."

They shifted their bags on their shoulders and began to cross.

"Under us, Drawyer River," said Bntno.

Lily looked down over the edge of the railing of the bridge. She could not see the river.

Instead, she saw something looking back up.

It had a thousand eyes. It was crawling up the wall. Mouths flapped open and shut, and chipped, yellow teeth clacked closed, gulping air.

Lily yelled a warning to the others, and they began to run—but the creature pulled itself up, towering like a column right next to the end of the bridge.

The eldritch demon-spawn yawned and smacked over the pit, hungering for sacrifice. It swayed and waited and unfurled its tentacles to pluck at prey. Flights of black and orange butterflies flittered before it, rising past the tiger lilies on the cliffs.

Everything was confusion. Bntno, rubber heels slapping at the stone, bolted right past to the other side and kept on going. Lily had made it too and lingered by the stairs. Jasper pointed his gun, shouted for Katie to just run past the thing—and he began to fire.

Jasper's gun was still out of juice, but he jiggled it, and he got a few darts of blue light to shoot out at the beast. The monster screamed from several mouths, bellowing like a pipe organ—waved its tentacles—and shot forward to grab Katie.

She battered the spongy arms with one of her bags.

Jasper shot another ray into the monster, its flesh sizzling. It sent a tentacle reeling at him, and he danced away, firing. The cavern flickered with hot, blue light.

The monster had tangled its grapplers in the straps of Katie's two packs. One of them—her own—was still on her shoulders, yanked by the monster. The other—which she'd been carrying for Jasper—was hurled into one of the monster's maws.

Katie struggled, she kicked, but she was being dragged toward the chasm—and toward the beast itself.

"Release the backpack straps!" Jasper yelled. "Katie! Katie!"

She ducked—she twisted—she turned. She fell. The wicked Thing hauled her toward its mouths. Black butterflies wobbled through the air before her face. She scraped over dirt and baby tears, wrestling with her own arms.

Jasper shot the Thing again. "Too weak!" he muttered, rattling his ray gun. Now the batteries were truly gone. The laser was just a feeble beam of light.

So, raising it once more, he aimed it directly at the Thing's eye. He fired. The gun flashed.

The Thing blinked. It twitched, then growled—but in the moment of that twitch,

Katie had hunched her back. She threw her arms above her.

She was free of her pack.

It slid toward the monster without her.

The Thing tossed the backpack in its mouth while Katie, half crawling, scrambled for the stairs.

Now they all started clattering upward, away from the pit and the eldritch Thing.

"Sorry, Jasper," said Katie, "I lost your extra supplies."

He looked a little guilty. He didn't say anything.

Lily glanced back down toward the Thing. It had pulled itself up and was starting to galumph after them, heavy blue-veined lips smearing against the rock.

"My ray-gun batteries are now entirely dead," said Jasper. "Do we have any other plans, chums?"

"Running," said Katie. "That seems like a plan."

There was a ferocious cry behind them. Stunned, they couldn't help but look back.

The ancient demon-spawn, child of a lost and awful world, was clutching its stomach. It was balled up and woozy.

"It must have eaten some . . ." Katie stopped herself. "Jasper," she said, "what was in that extra backpack? That backpack I've been carrying for two days now?"

He said, in a very small voice, "Why, supplies, Katie."

"Jasper?" she said. "What kind of supplies have I been carrying in that extra backpack for two days now, while being chased by cannibals, creatures from pits—and *allosauruses*?"

"Well, Katie, when your pluck is unplucked and your pep is—"

"*Jasperrrrr!*"

"Why, there's nothing that zaps up your zip like—"

"*Jasper Dash, have I been carrying sixteen twelve-ounce jars of Gargletine Instant Breakfast Drink through twenty-five miles of tropical rain forest?*"

"Yes, Katie."

"And why didn't you just tell me that I was carrying—"

"I was ashamed," said Jasper, "because you always make fun of Gargletine, and recently you haven't been doing anything but arguing with me about Delaware and laughing at me. You've been— Anyway . . . So I didn't want to show the jars to you. Because a fellow gets tired of being *ha-ha*'ed to death. To absolute death, Katie. Now argue with me about *that*."

"Um, Jas," said Katie, pointing down the stairs at the monster. "Maybe it's good I didn't drink any of that Gargletine."

The Thing writhed on the bottom steps. It held its stomach and groaned out of twelve mouths in uneasy, passing harmony. It shlupped itself toward its home pit like a daddy longlegs crawling off the windshield of a speeding car.

"Let's go," said Lily. "While it's slowed down."

"Yes," said Jasper, with dignity. "Because once the Gargletine takes effect, the Thing will be . . . much . . . stronger . . . and peppy . . . All Saturday long."

They climbed the stairs to freedom.

"I'm sorry, Jasper," said Katie. "It's just that right now—okay—I am a little sick of boys and their pride. It always seems like boys have got to be right about, you know, tyrannosauruses."

"Why, gee, no, Katie. I am sorry. Here I—"

"Moody guests," said Bntno, "perhaps we walk on upstairs and speak of tyrannosauruses when we don't have so many monster right behind us. Then heartwarming talk of friends and oh sorry and clasp hands, ta-da."

So they kept toiling up the steps leading out of the overgrown kingdom of Greylag.

And when they got to the top and stepped out of an old stone cupola, they found themselves on a beautiful plateau. The fronds and petals whispered in the breeze. The eyes of birds shone bright. The air was warm and friendly, curling on their arms and hair.

And over the peaceful scene, blocking out the thousand jillion stars and the Milky Way, dashed across this American landscape, were the shadows of four mountains rising from the hills. Bdreth, Minndfl, Tlmp, and Drgsl. They hunched like cowled monks surveying the world.

Katie, Jasper, and Lily looked in awe around them. On one of those mountains stood Vbngoom, the Platter of Heaven. Whichever one of them was Tlmp.

"They're beautiful," said Lily.

"Indeed," said Jasper. His voice full of awe, he said, "On one of those mountains, Drgnan Phglik waits for us. We are coming, my friend. We will soon be there." He asked Bntno, "Which one of them is Tlmp?"

Bntno was rooting around in his sack for his roast beef sandwich.

"Bntno?" said Lily.

"Yes, lovely guests?"

"Which one is Tlmp?" Jasper repeated.

"Yes?"

"Which mountain is Tlmp?"

"Which I-not-know is what?" said Bntno.

He took a bite out of his sandwich. "I am not very good with which-ways."

"But we need to know which mountain to go up," said Katie. "There are four of them."

"Yes, you choose. I do not know where monastery is. I get you here, but you take me to Vbngoom."

"It's on Mount Tlmp," said Jasper. "So which one is Tlmp?"

"One with Vbngoom on it."

"Thank you," said Jasper. "Swell. Tell me which of those four. The one farthest to the east? To the west? One of the ones in the middle?"

"Rocket-youngster does not see what is said to him. I am not know which mountain has which name. The story say that these mountains, they are dance when it cloudy. All . . ." He slapped his hands around next to each other to suggest the mountains changing places.

"Will we be able to see Vbngoom in the morning?" asked Katie. "On top of one of them?"

"Oh no," said Bntno. "Oh no. Can't see no

tops because of rumples. Vbngoom, it is very great secret of Delaware state." He finished with his sandwich, balled up the aluminum foil, and shoved it into a convenient blossom. "Time for sleep now. In morning, you will find monastery for us."

"Um," said Katie, "aren't you supposed to be our *guide*?"

"Shh! I am to be sleeping," said Bntno, shaking out his bedding and laying it on the ground.

And so, exhausted, not knowing where they'd be headed the next day, they unrolled their sleeping bags and fell asleep in the vale between the four great star-shadows of the four greatest peaks in the greatest mountain range in the state of Delaware.

44

Up on one of those mountaintops, locked in the board game and tiger closet of Vbngoom, Platter of Heaven, young Drgnan Pghlik crouched next to Nrrrgarha, monastery pet, waiting to be eaten.

So far, Drgnan had not been clawed. He had not been mauled or bitten.

The tiger knew him. They had lived together for years. Still, this was a tiger, not a calico cat with a love of sunbeams and people smooshing their face in his fur singing about bouncy mice and shnuggles. Nrrrgarha was a beast of the wild. He hunted the slopes in lean times.

Drgnan talked to the tiger as he had been taught, speaking gently, compassionately, and evenly, freeing them both from all desires. He asked the tiger to look within. He told the tiger to forget worldly hungers, for worldly hungers are the crooked stick with which wickedness thwacks us.

At first, Nrrrgarha was lulled by the sound of Drgnan's voice.

But hours passed—days, probably—and now Nrrrgarha was getting restless. He no longer purred when curled next to Drgnan. He fidgeted. And after a few days in the game closet, Drgnan smelled unwashed, and he knew the tiger was thinking about meat.

So Drgnan started to think again about escape.

Of course, he had tried several things already. He had attempted to unscrew the hinges. No luck. He had searched the closet for something he could saw with or scratch away at the bottom of the door with. No luck.

But now he had a new idea.

Carefully, he reached across Nrrrgarha to the shelf where the games were stored.

The tiger growled at him. The growl was irritable. Like he might just swipe at the boy.

"Consider a still, peaceful place," said Drgnan. "Nrrrgarha, listen to me. Picture a mountain pool."

The tiger growled.

"With a caribou in it."

The tiger growled louder.

Drgnan had a box in his hand. He drew it over to him. The box sagged and torqued in the air over the tiger's head.

Drgnan lay the box on his lap. Carefully, he removed the lid and felt the contents.

He felt the grain of the board . . . some cards . . . a pile of fake money . . . and yes, houses, many small houses . . .

Monopoly. Monastic Monopoly. He felt triumphant, as if he'd just bought the Water Works, Westminster Abbey, and the Vatican, and built a line of hotels straight across them.

Slowly he picked up the stack of cards. He slid one under the door, keeping the corner of it under his finger.

Now he needed something to poke with.

Here was his plan: He knew the key was still

in the keyhole. He could poke it from his side so it would fall out on the other side. It would land on the Monopoly card. Then he would draw the card slowly back under the door, bringing the key with it. Then he would unlock himself, and he and Nrrrgarha would be free.

But he needed something to poke the key with. He groped through the Monopoly box. For a second, he thought maybe the die-cast metal top hat or the 1930s roadster would do the trick, but the car's running boards were too wide. It didn't fit in the keyhole.

He lay the Monopoly game aside and reached back over to the shelf.

He came up with Travel Scrabble. Because it was the Doverian edition, it had hardly any vowels.

Then another long box. He lifted it over to him. He laid it on his knees.

Nrrrgarha stirred restlessly.

Drgnan prowled around the board. Little holes, with . . .

ZAP! There was a red light—a bulb—and Nrrrgarha rose to his feet, snarling.

It was Operation, Drgnan realized. An old game where you try to remove body parts with tweezers. The patient's nose lights up when you get it wrong. Drgnan had knocked the metal tweezers against the metal edge near the funny bone.

He didn't really want to think about anyone removing body parts at the moment.

Nrrrgarha stood in the darkness, growling deep in his throat.

Young Drgnan Pghlik reminded himself that his heart must be as still as a pat of wolf-butter on a hot cinnamon bun. He cleared his mind of tigers. Though one stood two feet from him, showing its fangs in the darkness.

Stifling his fear, Drgnan lifted the tweezers out of the game box. He felt for the door handle. He inserted the tweezers in the keyhole and inched them forward.

"You are a fine tiger," he said to his hungry

companion. "You are a prince of tigers. The stars themselves marvel at your serenity."

The tweezers hit the key.

Gently, Drgnan shoved.

The key slid.

The key fell.

He heard the clatter as it hit the Monopoly card and the floor.

Nrrrgarha's snarl had slowed to an angry ticking.

Drgnan eased the card toward him under the door. The key was there. . . . It was almost under . . . almost . . . almost . . . al—

It hit against the bottom of the door. There wasn't enough space. It couldn't fit. He slid it one way and then the other. No dice. It didn't fit. It just didn't.

The light in the next room snapped on.

"Hey! Hey! Look at this!"

Movement of shoes.

"Kid in a dress is trying to escape."

Despair hit Drgnan hard. The tiger still

bridled. The gangsters knew he was trying to get out. His plan had failed.

He pulled the card back under the door. The one the key had rested on.

In the faint light from the other room, he could just read it. It said, GET OUT OF JAIL FREE.

No such luck.

The tiger paced in the shadows, waiting.

45

Lily was awakened by something around dawn. She thought it was someone sneaking, or maybe talking. She lay very still and listened to the morning sounds. The dawn chorus of birds was singing. The bushes and trees were loud with them.

Finally Lily decided that the sound had been her imagination. Still, she was awake. She thought she would get up and watch dawn rise over the Four Peaks. Carefully she unzipped her sleeping bag partway—the zip trundling slowly, tooth by tooth, down the seam. She folded back a triangle, pulled her legs out, and rose.

She had not gone two steps, however, when Katie stirred and whispered, "Hey! Lily! Are you up?"

"Yeah," said Lily.

"One sec," said Katie, and she also got up. Jasper and Bntno didn't move.

Katie and Lily walked a little ways away from the camp and sat on a hill of grasses, watching the sky lighten. The grasses waved around them. The sky went from navy to a strange, simmering white.

The mountains turned red with the first sun.

Lily thrilled at the sight of that dawning. It seemed to her like the world was beginning again, like there was something pure and fresh about things. It didn't matter, somehow, that most walls were covered with dirt and that people punched each other in the lunch line. There was hope for the world, she felt, so long as there were mountains and forests and morning light.

Soon they could see the features that Jasper had mentioned on the mountains: the one farthest from them coated in white glacier; another with a lake on it, surrounded by grasses and trees; another draped in a deep pine forest; and a final one, with only occasional thickets on it, but with a giant pillar that could be seen from their roost several miles distant.

"So we don't know which one is which?" said Katie.

"No," said Lily.

"And Jasper really doesn't know? He's not just being a pain?"

"He was unconscious when he was taken up Tlmp."

"So what are we going to do?" said Katie. "We don't even know where we're going anymore. And we may be being followed."

Lily thought about it. They watched flocks of white birds soar above the forest. They watched a distant family of mountain goats—just brown specks on the rough stones—jump along the mountain trails.

Suddenly Lily said, "I have an idea."

"Really?"

"Yeah. I just realized—I think we might be able to figure out which mountain is which."

Katie looked at her. "Okay," said Katie. "Be my guest."

46

Lily ran back down the hillock to the camp. She carefully fished out the *There and Back Again*™ *Guide to Greater Delaware* from Jasper's pack. She also took a notebook and a pen.

Bntno was muttering in his sleep as usual. His pillow was over his head. Jasper was snoring slightly, his arms sprawled in the grass. Lily left them and made her way back to Katie's side.

"Okay," said Lily. "I wonder if we can't work out which mountain is which through deduction." She flipped open the notebook. She thumbed through the *There and Back Again*™. She passed it to Katie. "Read this part out loud again," she said.

Katie looked at a couple of the pictures on the page—both of women sitting smiling on top of heaps of grain—and then read: " 'Though the Four Peaks look the same height, trekkers will find that Mount Minndfl is actually considerably shorter than the nearby peak covered with deceptively inviting pine woods. English explorer and adventurer Leslie Arbuckle-Smythe climbed both that forested peak—despite its imposing height—and Mount Bdreth because he was too superstitious to climb near the ancient, rune-inscribed pillar that stands on one of the other mountains.' "

"Okay?" said Lily.

"Okay," said Katie. "What now?"

"We have four mountains. Called?"

"I don't know," said Katie. "They all sound like someone hawking loogies into a metal trash can."

Lily leaned over and read the guidebook over her friend's shoulder. She said, "Tlmp, Bdreth, Drgsl, and Minndfl."

"Right. Loogies."

Lily said, "So now let's write down what we know about them."

She wrote (and read):

"1. The monastery of Vbngoom is on top of Tlmp.

2. Lesley Arbuckle-Smythe climbed Mount Bdreth and the mountain with the pine forest because he was too superstitious to climb the mountain with the pillar.

3. Mount Minndfl is shorter than the mountain with the pine forest."

"Okay," said Katie. "Now I'm completely confused."

"So am I," said Lily. "So let's try this." On her tablet, she made a kind of tic-tac-toe grid, four columns by four rows. Across the top, in each column, she wrote the name of one of the mountains: *Drgsl*, *Bdreth*, *Tlmp*, and *Minndfl*. Then she continued, "Okay. Now, we have four mountains in front of us: the pillar mountain, the lake mountain, the pine mountain, and the glacier mountain. And we have to figure out which is which." In the rows going down, Lily wrote *pillar*, *lake*, *pine forest*, and *glacier*. Her chart looked like this:

	Drgsl	Bdreth	Tlmp	Minndfl
pillar				
lake				
pine forest				
glacier				

"Now, we can try to figure out which mountain is which by a process of elimination." Lily looked at the clues for a minute and then thought out loud. "Okay. Okay. We know from clue number two that Mount Bdreth is *not* the mountain with the pine forest *or* the mountain with the pillar."

"How?"

"Because it says that this man climbed Mount Bdreth *and* the mountain with the pine forest *instead of* the mountain with the pillar. So Mount

Bdreth must not be either of them. So we write *X*'s in the Bdreth column, next to *pillar* and *pine forest*. Because Bdreth can't be either one." She scribbled down the *X*'s, so her chart looked like this:*

	Drgsl	Bdreth	Tlmp	Minndfl
pillar		X		
lake				
pine forest		X		
glacier				

---

*You can also follow along and detect while Lily does. That's what I'm doing, because I'm completely lost.

Take a crayon, a quill, or a jagged inky stick. Make a grid like Lily's. Write *X*'s in the spaces when you absolutely know that a particular description *doesn't* fit one of the mountain names. And write an O in the space when you know that a particular description *does* fit a particular mountain name. Follow along, and see if you can guess it first!

"Oh, yeah . . . ," said Katie. "Now it's too bad we don't know the heights of the different mountains, because then maybe we could figure out which one is Mount Minndfl."

"We don't need to know the heights," said Lily. "That third clue at least tells us that Mount Minndfl is *not* the pine mountain. So we put an *X* where the Minndfl column meets the pine mountain row."

"So what do we have?"

"Well, Mount Tlmp could be any of them . . . so can Mount Drgsl. Mount Bdreth could be either the lake or glacier. And Mount Minndfl could be the glacier, the lake, or the pillar."

Katie looked at this set of clues, her interest clearly piqued. "Hmm," she said. "We need to know more."

"We need another clue," said Lily.

Luckily they were not living in a world where there are rarely enough clues, and we wander around sadly in our trench coats, kicking at tired grass in empty lots as the greasy rain falls. They were in a book where the final clue always comes to you, and you snap, and say—

Lily snapped. "I've got it!" she said. "I just thought of something!"

"Uh-huh?" said Katie.

"The menu at that restaurant we went to had deep-fried Mount Drgsl Squid on it!"

"You're not talking about breakfast, are you?"

"No—so there must be water on Mount Drgsl. *Mount Drgsl must be the mountain with the lake on it!*"

Katie's mouth was open. "Oh, yeah!" she said, with admiration in her voice. "Yeah! Because the squid's there! Write that down!"

"Okay," said Lily, looking over her notes. "So we know that Mount Drgsl is the lake. I can put an O there. That means that . . ." (She crossed things out.) "Mount Bdreth, which we said could be either the glacier or the lake *can't* be the lake. The lake is ruled out. So Mount Bdreth must be the glacier . . ."

Katie leaned over to look at the notebook, grabbing Lily's shoulder. "And that means that Mount Minndfl must be the pillar!"

"*And so Mount Tlmp—,*" said Lily—and they both exclaimed together, "*must be the mountain with the pine forest on it!*"

They gave each other a high five.

They looked up at Tlmp, towering above them, the peak snaring clouds.

"Jasper will be so excited!" said Lily.

"Yeah," said Katie. "I feel kind of bad for being a jerk to him."

"He understands," said Lily.

"That I'm a jerk?"

"No, you're not a jerk," said Lily. "You're a wonderful friend."

"Not always."

Lily smiled. "You saved me from cannibals."

Katie thought about this. "Oh," she said. "Oh, yeah. The cannibals. I think I just pulled on your arm a lot."

"That was good," said Lily.

"The cannibals would have pulled on your arm too. Except they would have had buffalo-style hot sauce on it."

"Your pulling kept me running. And you slowed down your own running for me. So I wouldn't fall behind."

"No I didn't."

"You know you did."

"Lily . . ."

"I know I'm slow."

"You're not slow."

"I'm kind of slow. Thank you for slowing down."

"Can we not make this into one of those conversations where everyone talks about how pathetic they are?" said Katie. She stood up. "Let's go wake up the boys and tell them we've figured out where the monastery is."

They grinned at each other.

Together they ran down the hill and toward the camp.

When they got there, both Jasper and Bntno were still in their sleeping bags. Bntno was still muttering under his pillow.

Katie tiptoed over and prepared to seize

Jasper by the shoulders and wake him up with a start, screaming, "Fire!" She stood with her fingers massaging the air.

Then she looked up at Lily. Lily had walked near Bntno's sleeping bag and was frozen strangely in place. Lily put her finger to her lips.

So Katie was very quiet when she reached down and shook Jasper and whispered, "Jas . . . Hey, Jas, we figured out which mountain is which."

She looked again at Lily for approval. Lily was frantically waving her hands and shaking her head. Lily pointed to Bntno's sleeping bag.

Katie didn't know what was going on, but she froze. They both listened.

"Come in, Ministry of Silence . . . ," Bntno was muttering. "Here, Agent Bntno . . . Ministry of Silence, please come in . . ."

Bntno was a spy!

47

"Agent Bntno . . . This, Agent Bntno . . . We are at Four Peaks. . . . Yes, you hears me? We are at Four Peaks. . . ."

Lily stood absolutely still, wondering what to do. They would somehow have to lose Bntno before they continued on their way! Otherwise, he would report the whereabouts of the monastery to the government, and the Awful and Adorable Autarch of Dagsboro would plunder its remaining treasures and use its powers for tyrannical evil.

"Children have made it to Four Peaks," whispered Bntno. "Tonight, I will—"

"Alley-oop!" exclaimed Jasper, raising himself up on one elbow. "Katie, were you about to grab me roughly and startle me awake?" He smiled. "You have to get up pretty early to surprise Jasper Dash."

Katie covered her face with her hands. Lily stood up straighter.

Bntno stopped talking in his sleeping bag. He cleared his throat.

"The excellent children are awake?" Bntno said, sticking his head out. "I have very strange dream where I talk out loud. Very strange dream."

"Did I hear," said Jasper loudly, "that you two have figured out which mountain is which?"

Katie frowned. Lily waved her hands.

"Well?" said Jasper. "Drop the soup, chums! Which is it? Where's the monastery? I'm ready as an evergreen to spread my limbs up to the sun and say, 'Hello, happy morning!'" He stretched and crawled out of his sleeping bag.

Katie and Lily didn't say anything.

Bntno looked a little suspicious. "You know which mountain?" asked Bntno. "How instructive!"

"Which is it, then?" said Jasper.

Katie rocked on her heels. "We don't know," she said. "We didn't figure it out."

"What's the fuss, then?" said Jasper.

"I think they knows," said Bntno. "They are the joking people; they not tell us for joke. But now joke over. Now they tell."

Lily and Katie looked at each other desperately. How were they going to warn Jasper? How were they going to get rid of Bntno before he found out what they knew and reported it to the government?

"We really don't know," said Lily.

"Nope," said Katie. "We are as dumb as coal."

Bntno smiled widely. He stepped out of his sleeping bag. In one hand was a small walkie-talkie-like thing: his two-way radio. In the other hand was a gun. "The girls know somethings," he said. "They know I maybe tell a thing or another thing to Ministry of Silence. But it is time now for talking. Yes? It is time now to tell."

Bntno pointed the gun at Lily. "Tell us. Which mountain is monastery of Vbngoom on?

301

We would like to go there with helicopter. Make the monks salute our Terrifying and Awful Adorable Autarch. Get some magic powers for our Ministry of Silence. You tell us. Tell us where it is."

"Don't, Lily," said Jasper. "The monastery is depending on you."

Lily looked straight down the barrel of Bntno's gun.

48

And then there was a crackle in the bushes. And another voice with a Doverian accent said, "Puts gun down! Puts gun down!"

Lily was confused. It was as if a prompter for a play was calling out the stage directions. She felt like she was hallucinating. But the voice came again. "All of you! No gun! Stand up! Hand up!"

A man stepped out of the bushes. He had a gun, too. He was wearing camouflage clothing.

"You've been following us!" cried Jasper.

"Puts gun down!" said the man.

Bntno slowly crouched and lay his pistol on the grass. He stood back up, his hands raised above his head.

"Thank you!" said Katie. "We were just thinking that he was going to—"

"Quiet silence!" cried the new gunman.

Katie and Lily had no idea what was going on. Jasper, I'm afraid, did.

"Sir," he said, "I know what this is about."

"You!" said the man. "Yes, you!"

"Who is this person?" asked Katie.

"Fifteen cent!" said the man. "Fifteen cent!"

"Ah," said Jasper Dash. "Yes, I owe you fifteen cents. I deeply apologize. You very generously let me use your commuter vaultapult to chase—"

"I follow you days! I get that fifteen cent!"

Jasper smiled. "Indeed. And you've saved us again. We are very grateful to you. Of course, I shall pay what I owe you down to the last penny. May I put down my hands and get the change for you?"

The man nodded angrily.

Jasper reached down and felt in his pockets.

While he searched, Lily asked quietly, "Why didn't you just stop us early on? Why did you follow us?"

"Whenever I find you, you is always sleeped."

"You could have woken us up," said Katie.

"Very rude! No. I will not wake up the peoples. I not rude. This sir, he is rude." The man gestured at Jasper.

"But you were fine with putting sugar in our gas tank," said Katie.

"To stop you! But you are not stop! So next night, I catch up, I finds you, I come to speak to you, and you are snoozed again! I do not want to be rude man. So I try to write message to you: 'Remember you owe me fifteen cent—'"

"But your Magic Marker ran out of ink," said Lily.

"Yes! Bad for write on metal door."

The Boy Technonaut was searching the pockets of his rucksack. He said, "I'm glad that this is all that the following business was about. It was getting quite worrying. Anyway, ha. Swell. Let me just . . ." His hands came up empty. Nothing. "Chums," he said, "perhaps you have the fifteen cents?"

Lily started to check her jeans.

"Don't," said Katie. "Bother. Don't bother." She sounded kind of miserable.

"Why?" said Jasper. "Surely one of us has . . ." And then he realized.

"Nope," said Katie. "I . . . um . . . I used all of our change to try to buy a Dr Pepper back at that base."

"Every . . . penny . . . ," Jasper realized.

"Yeah," said Katie. "Every last little penny."

"Then," said their stalker, "then thing end very badly right now. Very badly, yes. I take one of you with me as hostage. And now I get very rude, too."

He raised his gun.

49

"You," he said to Bntno. "Man with gun. You come with me as hostage."

Bntno pointed to himself.

"Yes. Man with gun. Now. I pick up you gun. And you walk with me. We walk back to Dover. And you find me change, fifteen cent."

"But I—"

"*The gun speak louder than the talk!*" screamed the vaultapult attendant. "I have walk three day to come here. Make good speed!"

Bntno slowly and sadly gathered up his sleeping bag and his backpack. The man kept the gun on him. The man told Jasper and Lily how to tie Bntno's hands.

Then the man led Bntno away into the jungle,

Bntno complaining, in Doverian, that the Ministry of Silence would be peeved.

Soon they were gone.

For a while, the three friends stood where they were, kind of shocked. So much had changed so quickly.

The birds tootled and sang.

"Great Scott," said Jasper. "I think we just had two problems solved at once."

"Yeah . . . ," said Katie. "I . . . guess."

"So you know which mountain the monastery is on?"

"Sure," said Katie. "That one." She pointed at the mountain with the pine forest.

"Oh," said Jasper. He clapped his hands together briskly. "Well," he said, "it's an excellent day for a walk, we have miles to go, and a friend awaits us at the end of the road. Have I mentioned that I feel like a redwood about to spread its limbs toward the sun?"

"And say to the morning, 'Hello,' " said Lily.

50

Later that afternoon, the three friends reached the great pine forests of Tlmp. Though the day was still warm, a chill wind beat at them as they climbed up through its heights. The boughs of the pines swayed, sending deep shadows skating across their faces.

"Who would have thought this weekend, when we were at the big game, that a few days later we'd be climbing a mountain looking for a monastery?" said Lily.

"Yeah," grumbled Katie. "Who would've thought." She sighed and spread out her steps to crunch a pinecone at each footfall. "At least," she said, "I haven't thought about Choate Brinsley all day."

"Choate?" said Jasper. "Why are you trying not to think about Choate?"

"Jasper," said Katie pityingly. "You really don't understand, do you?" She hopped to crush a cone.

He furrowed his brow. "You puzzle me, Katie."

"You know, sometimes, there's this attraction that can't be explained?"

"Are you speaking of gluons and quarks? Certainly they can't be explained entirely by current physics, but I hope that through the application of my antimatter accelerator—"

"That's not what I mean," said Katie.

"An antimatter accelerator sounds a little dangerous," said Lily.

"Yeah," said Katie. "Who ever needed fast antimatter?"

"You are speaking," Jasper intuited, "of the tender sentiments."

Katie said, "Whoo-boy."

"Yes, Jasper," said Lily. "That's kind of what she's talking about."

"You have a pash for Choate Brinsley?"

"A what?"

"A crush?"

"I did. He's always mean to me."

"So you've stopped having a crush on him?"

"It's not really that simple."

Jasper said, "Surely you can't want to spend time with someone who is mean to you."

"Well, he wouldn't be mean to me if we were going out."

Lily said, "You don't know that."

"We could ride a tandem bicycle," said Katie. "And go for canoe rides in the summer."

"Katie," said Jasper, "you're too good a person for Choate Brinsley. The girls he likes . . . They can't hold a candle to you. They're not funny like you are. They're not plucky like you are. They're not wonderful like you are. They have never stopped the hungry hauntings of zombies. They have never defeated a single toad god or had the pleasure of repelling gunplay with a trash-can lid."

Katie felt her throat getting all wobbly. "Thank

you, Jas," she said. After a minute of walking in silence, with Katie crunching on the pinecones, she said, "But you know, sometimes I kind of feel like I'd like to be normal. Maybe all three of us would be happier if we were more normal."

"No one's normal," said Lily quietly. "For people to be normal, there would have to be an average person. But people are too different. Look at all the people in Dover and then think about people back in Pelt. What's normal?"

"Exactly," Jasper said.

"Normal," said Katie, "means when you go out with your friends, you know you won't end the evening jumping over pits of talking carpenter ants."

"I apologize for that," said Jasper soberly. "But that was three weeks ago, and I wish we would all put it behind us."

"Do you think Choate would ever—"

I am very glad that the conversation was interrupted at this moment by a long tentacle coming down out of the trees, because I have to say I do not like emotional conversations.

312

The Cutesy Dell Twins' books are filled with talk about who likes who and whether people are "right" for each other. In each and every book of that series, one or the other of them falls in love with somebody and spends the whole time thinking about him in a T-shirt, riding a horse— but nothing ever really works out for them. The guy's cuter jerky cousin comes to town, or it turns out he's really someone's brother in disguise, or he moves to Cincinnati, or they have a disagreement about how to take care of dogs. Talk, talk, talk. No one stumbles on any ancient devices, the stars in the night sky are pretty and not filled with alien menace, and there is never a single circular saw—let alone a circular saw with a conveyor belt.

My friends, where's the zest in that?

No, give me a slice of the life adventurous. Show me something unusual. Give me the stuff of dreams and nightmares!

For example, this gigantic, many-eyed beast currently warping its way between the trees, grabbing at Katie with its tentacles. Now *that* is something to talk about. Would you rather we talked about the beast, with its thousand eyes and sloppy mouths and carking cries of hunger, or go back to "Is he right for me?" and "Oh, it's just like there's this fence between us and I can see between the pickets, but some are overgrown with this . . ." etc. etc.?

I know my answer. And I'll give it quick, because Katie might only have a few seconds left with her current arms and face.

Excuse me.

Okay: Roll the beast!

51

The beast swayed above them, its drooling mouths smacking, its tentacles snaking between the pine boughs. Its cries echoed over the crags and cliffs.

"Run!" said Jasper. "It's the Thing from the bridge in Greylag!"

They ran, bounding through spruce.

"I think," Lily said, puffing, "I think . . . this one's smaller."

"Or a child," said Jasper. "Of the same species."

The three swerved around bushes. The awful kraken levered itself over branches, chuckling in the firs.

"I have . . . a horrible thought . . . ," said Lily.

Katie asked, "What's that?" as the beast roared.

"The tentacles . . . ," said Lily. "Katie . . .

Jasper . . . Maybe these are mountain squids. I . . . thought they . . . lived in the water . . . but . . ."

"But maybe they don't," said Katie. "Maybe they live in trees and chasms."

"And . . . ," Lily panted, "that means . . . that we might be going up the wrong mountain . . . Maybe Tlmp . . . is the one with the lake . . ."

"We can't think about that just now," said Jasper.

"It's no good running!" said Katie, looking backward. "It's faster than we are!"

The squid came hurtling down at them. Lily ducked—Jasper yelped—

The monster threw itself through the treetops—chose Katie—snaked out a feeler.

Katie shrieked—then shouted in defiant surprise, "What is it"—swatting at the tentacle—"with me and tentacles these days?"*

---

*Dear Ask Stacey:
Why are tentacled things always trying to throttle me?
Yours,
Pestered in Pelt
P.S. Sometimes twice a day.

The squid lifted her from the ground. She half turned—as much as she could—feeling the muscle ripple around her, and saw the huge, chip-toothed mouth, the pulsing coils—

She screamed.

And out of the air, a curious beast flew.

It was a dinosaur—green—with a gentle face—four stumpy legs—two graceful, feathered wings—and a sparkly, soft mane of purple and pink. It descended from the sky to face the squid.

Katie looked up at it in wonder.

It roared fearsomely at the mountain squid. The squid, aghast, dropped Katie to the ground. It started whipping tentacles at the sky, flailing the tops of the trees. The dinosaur roared, reared.

Battle was joined. The giant drool-mouths of the squid chomped away at the air as feelers

Dear Pestered:
Like cats, many tentacled things can detect who dislikes them or is allergic. That's the person they head right toward, drooling. It might be that you, coming from the Horror Hollow area, have developed a particular aversion to monstrosities that especially attracts them. An old home remedy for movie monsters: Try twelve Sherman tanks, a fighter plane, and a plan that is crazy but that *just might work*. For planes, my mother recommends the F-35 Lightning II! Good luck!

slapped the beating wings of the sky-saur. Gilt feathers wafted through the air.

Katie stood by her friends, mouth open, watching the battle.

"It's . . . it's my dinosaur," she said. "That I made out of my Star-Wonder Glitter-Pony. They . . . they really exist."

"Incredible!" said Jasper.

"We'd better run," said Lily. "While we can."

"Hey!" said Katie. "Where is that stupid teacher? *He should not have made me redo that dinosaur project! I want an appeal to a higher court!*"

They had started walking away from the fight. Katie's dinosaur had lifted up the mountain squid, pulling its suckers out of the treetops, and was carrying it off somewhere for dinner.

"Um, we have another problem," said Lily. "If that's a mountain squid, then we don't know that we're even on the right mountain."

Katie asked, "Do you think that dinosaur

could become my own special dinosaur? And always protect me from tentacles?"

Jasper took his brass telescope out of his bag and trained it on the other peaks. "I am searching . . . ," he said, "searching for other monsters like that one. Ah. Yes. There's one crawling on the rocks near the giant pillar. And one in the grass near the lake. This is a dismal sight, chaps. The mountains appear to be fairly lousy with squid."

"So we don't know we're going the right way," said Lily. "I led us into a wild goose chase."

"No," said Jasper, snapping the spyglass shut. "*I* led us into a wild goose chase."

But it was Lily who felt awful. She had been proud of her solution—she felt like she had really contributed something—and she'd been proved wrong.

I know exactly how she feels. Because you and I were proved wrong too. We did the same puzzle and came up with the same solution. It could be that if we'd figured out that grid correctly, right now you'd be reading a book about someone on a different mountain, striding up to the mysterious, aeon-blasted pillar, say, and reaching out a hand to touch its pitted surface, when suddenly we hear, through the howling wind on the high heath, a sound like something moving right underground, under our feet, and realize that this mountain is actually the fabled location of—

But no. All of us—you, me, and Lily—have ended up here on the mountain with the pine forest, and our choice wasn't illogical. We did a good job. We just didn't know an important fact about mountain squids.

But still, Lily felt terrible. She scraped at the bangs that kept blowing in her eyes, and squinted bleakly around at the peaks and the jungles.

"What are we going to do?" said Katie.

"Let's keep going up," said Jasper. "When we have a better vantage point, maybe we'll be able to see the tops of the other mountains."

They walked through steep valleys of rock. They scrambled over bracken. There were, eventually, blueberry bushes.

Each time they thought they were almost at the peak of the mountain, they discovered that they were just on the lip of another hillock—and still the mountain towered higher.

Round about evening, they broke out of the tree line for good.

Below them, stretching as far as they could see, were the jungles of Delaware: the gorges and hills. Very far away they saw the grasslands, the rice paddies through which they had driven with Bntno. Out there lights were sparkling in distant villages and farmsteads.

The cold evening wind blew over them.

"We don't even know that this is the right mountain anymore," said Lily.

"We need to sleep," said Katie. "I'm tired."

"It's not safe," said Jasper.

"So what are we going to do?" Katie demanded. "We can't just walk until we fall over!"

"We need to keep walking," said Jasper.

"Says who?" Katie demanded. "This isn't a walk-ocracy."

"I'd really like to stop," said Lily. "I mean, I could go on, but . . ."

Katie repeated, "What are we going to do?"

And just at that moment, nearby, there was a soft green glow.

They turned and looked across the barren mountainside. Boulders and crevasses caught the light of the dying sun. The sky was red. One blasted, crooked little tree was red.

And beside it was the ghostly figure of a boy. He did not seem to see them but stood upon the mountainside as if keeping watch. He was green and translucent, and his robes rippled in the wind.

It looked as if he had been standing there playing sentinel since the ancient times. He looked out over the crimson horizon.

"Drgnan!" exclaimed Jasper. "Drgnan Pghlik!"

He ran toward his old friend.

52

"Drgnan!" Jasper said. "It is wonderful to see you! Even translucently!"

But the ghostly Drgnan Pghlik did not seem aware of Jasper. It simply turned and started pacing away up the mountain.

"It's his astral form!" said Jasper, delighted. "He sent his astral form to guide us the last few miles."

They scurried after the specter.

"Lily," whispered Katie. "Do you realize what this means? You were right all along! Tlmp *is* the mountain with the pine forest—and we're on it!"

Lily nodded. "Yeah," she said, feeling a little better.*

"She's right, Lily," said Jasper, scrambling over a boulder. "If it hadn't been for you, we'd be hours away. He never would have found us."

"Can we throw stuff through him?" asked Katie. "I mean, safely?"

No one answered her; and soon, they were all too exhausted with the climb to speak. The ghostly figure led them along paths through the night. In some places, there were secret stairs that had been carved into the rock. He drifted forward on narrow rims of stone.

It grew colder. Very cold. Incredibly cold. Their breath came out in puffs.

Drgnan Pghlik walked without turning, seemingly without ever noticing their presence.

---

*She should feel a lot better. I just checked out what's happening on Mount Minndfl—remember, the mountain with the pillar, where things sounded really interesting a few hours ago? Well, it's pitch-dark up there, and the pillar's standing all alone with a storm howling around it, and there's no sign of any life at all, except the whooping of the mountain-squids farther down the slope. I wouldn't go there right now if you gave me three shiny nickels and the laces from your boots.

He led them through hollows of granite. They walked past cairns—piles of stones heaped on the top of cliffs. They passed old carvings: fanged faces, dancing gods.

A mist closed thickly around them. They were in the clouds. All they could see was Drgnan's glow. They shined their flashlights up and down the narrow path. Though they could not see the impossible drop to one side of them, they could hear it. They could feel it in the booming wind.

Lily thought she had never been so tired. She tried to concentrate on every step—not on how far they had left to go or how far they had come. One foot in front of another.

Her back hurt. Her head was sore. She was getting a throat-ache. Her hands were numb.

Jasper skipped along as if nothing was difficult for him, as if the air weren't condensing on them all as frost.

Through the night they climbed. It was a dark night, a night of haze and cold.

At around four o'clock, the mists began to clear.

They were climbing a long ridge of stone on all fours. Lily did not want the light to rise too quickly. She knew that she would see sheer drop-offs on either side of them. She didn't want to know. She didn't want to see how far she would fall if she slipped.

Snow blew across her face. She wiped it away, blowing her frozen bangs out of her eyes.

"Drgnan!" she heard Jasper call. "Drgnan? Where are you going?"

With the dawn, the specter was flickering out.

Drgnan Pghlik's astral form turned once, his forlorn face finally beseeching them for help. Then he disappeared.

"Drgnan! You can't leave us like this!" said Jasper. "Which way? Which way?"

Katie and Lily looked on in horror. But Jasper's friend was gone.

With the dawn, a great wind arose. A huge fan of snow swept across them and dissipated.

"Look!" said Katie. *"Look!"*

53

It stood above them, about a half mile away, lit bright against a blue sky and dazzling plumes of snow.

The monastery was built upon the craggy walls of a volcanic crater, crowning three little peaks, its bastions and bridges cast between them. It was a maze of sloping walls and stone towers, gardens of gemlike green and ornaments of brass dazzling in the morning sun—white stone and gilded spoons on which monks hurled themselves from temple to temple.

It rose up out of a pine wood, through which paths wound, lined with gray prayer flags flapping in the breeze. From the high battlements, the morning horns sounded.

Katie, Jasper, and Lily had reached Vbngoom, the Platter of Heaven.

PART FOUR

THE DRASTIC MONKS OF MBNGOOM

54

The three made their way toward the monastery. They were glad that their approach was hidden by the forest. They knew things would be very dangerous for them once they got close to the walls.

"Bobby Spandrel," said Jasper, "is clever and ruthless. We must take every precaution." He took out his ray gun and proceeded with it at the ready.

"Jasper," said Lily. "One thing with taking precautions? Just to remember?"

"Yes, Lily?"

"Your ray gun is out of batteries."

Jasper frowned. He pointed the gun straight up and fired it. Not even a flicker came out of the nozzle.

"You're right," he said. "Curses." He fired uselessly a few more times at the sky. "Ah well. Forward, chums."

"Forward," muttered Katie.

They walked down the path. On each side of them, there were gray prayer flags, thin and gauzy as ash, blowing in the mountain breeze.

They crept through thickets of spruce. Ahead of them, they could hear the sound of engines and groaning. They didn't like it at all.

They rested for a minute against three pillars they found in a clearing, and they planned in whispers.

"We don't have any weapons," said Jasper. "Not a single electro-atomic ray blaster among us. This worries me."

"How are we going to get into the monastery?" asked Katie. "We can't just walk up to the front gates."

"It's too bad we can't dress like monks," said Lily. "If we had . . . you know, monk suits."

"In movies," said Katie, "when people need to get into a secret facility, they always run into three guards and then they grab them and pull them off-screen into closets for a second and then they come out wearing their uniforms. And the uniforms are always exactly the right size. Maybe they pull them into fitting rooms."

Lily and Jasper really had nothing to say to this, so Katie continued, "Which would be great, except my feet are a really weird shape. I have a short foot, like a size five, but wide. It would be really hard to find a guard shoe that would—"

"Um, hey," whispered Lily.

She pointed straight up.

The others looked up at the top of the three pillars they were resting against.

Sitting on top of the pillars were three old monks, naked except for white loincloths. Their eyes were closed. Their beards had grown down and intermingled with their knees, their toes, and vines.

"Great Scott!" said Jasper. "Hermits!"

"What are they doing?" said Katie.

"Meditating! That's Brother Klrt! That would mean . . . he's been atop that pillar for almost forty years!"

"Then," whispered Lily, "he and the other two might not be needing these." She pulled three green robes and capes out of the bushes where they had been hanging.

"Swell!" cried Jasper. "Perfect!"

"Yuck," said Katie. "There's bird doo on one of them."

"Where?" said Lily, holding out the fabric and flipping it back and forth.

"On one of the hermits." Katie was still craning her neck to check out the tops of the pillars. "I think it's pigeons."

"Brother Svbnm was always a friend to the animals," Jasper recalled. "He had a chummy way with squirrels that kept him in tetanus shots for years."

Lily handed robes and capes to her friends.

As it happened, the clothes fit the three kids precisely. They hid their packs in the bushes.

As they fastened the chains that held on their capes, Jasper paused.

"What's wrong?" asked Katie.

Jasper hesitated. He said, "Remembering the past is sometimes a joyful and a sad thing at the same time."

"I know what you mean," said Katie.

"What are you remembering?" asked Lily.

"All the happy months. Chasing butterflies in these woods. My friend Drgnan Pghlik and I whistling chants and carving yak-butter sculptures. Singing evensong. Going to bed early to the sound of the monastery gong. Sleeping soundly in my horsehair nightgown. Rising early, as the conch shells were blown on the mountaintops and running downstairs through the cold hallways to a bath of hot coals . . ."

"Hot coals?" exclaimed Lily.

"Maybe the memory takes away the pain," said Jasper.

"It must be hard for you," said Katie, "knowing that your friends are in trouble because of your archenemy."

Jasper looked down at the forest floor and nodded. "Yes," he said. "This is my fight, not Vbngoom's. Bobby Spandrel has lured me here. Now it's time for me to show him that I stick by my friends."

"Don't worry, Jasper," said Lily. "We'll stick by our friend, too." She put her hand on his.

Jasper smiled weakly. "Thank you, Lily." He cleared his throat. "Well. Let's be off, shall we?"

Katie asked, "Are you sure it's okay to take these clothes?"

"I am sure that the three brethren wouldn't mind," said Jasper. "Their minds are on deeper things than mere clothes. Hip, hip, and away!"

The three, now clad as monks, slipped off into the wood, leaving the clearing empty. Katie's voice echoed back, saying, "It's a good thing they don't wear shoes, because it would be really hard to find a girl's size five wide in the . . ."

Birds sang in the hemlock trees and spruce. Butterflies wandered past. A deer walked through the clearing, browsing on moss.

The deer heard a movement and bounded off into the woods.

Up on top of the pillars, one of the monks had moved. His long beard flexed around his knuckles.

He stretched a scrawny arm and yawned. Twigs and acorns dribbled to the forest floor from his fists and pits.

"Okeydokey," he said in Doverian. "Hey! Hey, guys! Time's up!"

Lids fluttered. The other two monks awoke. "Huh?" said one. "What's up?"

"Time's up," said Klrt. "That makes forty years. On the button. On the nose. We're done."

"Oh, great," said Svbnm, rolling his head from side to side to crack his neck. "I could really use a glass of orange Tang and some baked beans."

"All righty," said Klrt, standing up on his pillar. "Let's go down and . . . Hey. Hey! Where's our . . . Hey! Whoa! Some joker stole our stuff! We can't go back to the monastery like this! Where's . . ."

Meanwhile, the three monks' clothes, with kids in them, crept closer to the sound of engines and groaning.

55

Under the towers and temples of Vbngoom was a sheer wall of granite blocks, raised up five hundred years before to repel the invasion of white-haired reavers from the frosty fastnesses of Winterthur.

Painted upon that wall was the ferocious chicken, guardian of the monastery, the symbol of the Realm of Delaware: blue, three-eyed, scream-beaked, and with a hundred wings and legs, each clutching a different weapon as if to say: *Puny mortal! Wish you to be smote by my drumsticks? Seek not my tenders!*

The ancient paint upon that wall was faded.

Faded, too, was the power of the monks. They now worked at the base of the wall while mobsters watched. The monks had been ordered to help build a road so the mobsters could drive right up to the gates of this new hideout, instead of parking near the bottom of the mountain. Robed men staggered along in lines, carrying rocks to lay as pavement. Their green robes were torn and black with grit. As they marched dolefully along, they sang a ragged chant in Latin to keep up their spirits. Chants in Latin are normally one of the only things that can cheer up a monk, but in this case, it sounded so slow and heartsick, it was more like a groan. The monks, even little kid monks, were bowed low beneath the weight of stone.

The road almost reached the front gates of the monastery.

A white van was parked on the new cobbles.

Crouched in the bushes, Jasper was aghast. "I can't believe they're building a road. Can't they let anything alone? Can't anything be cut off from anything else? Can't anything be lost?"

Lily knew what he meant. She loved places that people had forgotten, like the old gas station rotting on the edge of the forest in Pelt, all gray wood and brown metal. She liked to walk there sometimes and imagine that during tempests the king of the forest, dry leaves swirling around his motorcycle, would skid to a halt and demand unleaded gas from shadowy attendants while a mossy-faced knight sat in his sidecar.

Everyone has those places we know about and no one else knows: maybe a tunnel you pass in the subway that's never used anymore, or maybe a room in your school you find once and can never find again, or maybe just a little group of trees you see every day from the bus and have never been to but where you imagine something magical might happen. . . . And then one day, you go by that stand of trees, and you discover they've put a Planet Liquor store there, and the grand opening is Tuesday, but you miss the little tiny wood you knew because you miss the dreams it inspired.

This is how Jasper felt. Gazing up at the fortifications, he mused, "That wall withstood the flaming arrows of the barbarian bandits of Winterthur, nigh on five hundred years ago. The bandits learned to fear the chicken. And yet now—now common mobsters have broken into the peaceful calm of the monastery. It is a sad day, chums."

"So what are we going to do?" asked Katie. "Because the mobsters don't look like they fear the chicken."

"We could wait until they send some monks into the gates," said Lily. "Then we could just walk out and follow them in."

An oddly dressed figure caught their attention. In the middle of the line of male monks was one woman. She was wearing a fleece jacket, dirty prayer scarves, and hiking pants that could zip off at the knee to make shorts.

Lisa Buldene.

She was also carrying rocks. She looked very tired. Even the dye in her hair looked tired.

She said to everyone she passed, "You know, this is really withering my spirit. Don't think I won't call someone to complain. Because this is completely dimming the light of my joy."

"Keep your pants on, New York," said one of the mobsters. "I don't want to hear no guff."

"Someone from the tourist board is going to hear about this," said Lisa Buldene. "I didn't come here to haul rocks. I came here to find myself, and I don't expect—"

"You are gonna find yourself six feet underground, lady, if I do not commence hearing the delicious sound of silence right about nowish."

Lisa Buldene trudged on. Her head hung. She stopped complaining.

"Poor Lisa Buldene," said Katie.

Lily couldn't agree more. She imagined Lisa Buldene seeking this place she had dreamed of, finding it somehow, this hidden vale, these towers around this sacred crater—and then being immediately captured by mobsters and forced to carry rocks. Lily thought it must have been terrible for Lisa Buldene, to have her dreams smashed like that.

"The monks are just as innocent as her," said

344

Jasper. "There's no reason any of them deserve this." With a look of defiance in his eyes, he said, "It's me Bobby Spandrel wants." He frowned. "And it's me Bobby Spandrel is going to get."

With that, Jasper Dash walked out of the bushes toward the towering gates.

The other two rushed after him.

Jasper saw that the gates had been opened so a work party could file inside. He followed after them, not so close as to look like one of their number, but close enough so the doors wouldn't shut before he and his friends got inside.

The gates were fifteen feet high, set in the blank stone wall. They were guarded by mobsters with machine guns.

The long line of monks with rocks disappeared into the gates. Pulling their hoods low, Lily, Katie, and Jasper followed after.

The shadows swallowed them.

They were inside.

56

A wide passageway led up through the cliffs.
It was lit by torches in brackets on the wall. The
monks struggled along. Hanging back just slightly
were three shorter monks. One of them—Katie—
wobbled at every step because the rocks hurt her
bare feet. Lily was worried Katie would give herself
away. Lily had figured out how to arch her feet so
she wouldn't lurch around in pain, and Jasper didn't
seem bothered at all.

They came back out into the sunlight. They
were in a courtyard. The doors were all of shining brass, and banners flapped in the mountain
winds.

Jasper, Katie, and Lily were about to cut
away from the line of monks when they stopped
dead in their tracks.

There were Team Mom, Coach, and the seven remaining Stare-Eyes players, talking in a group.

"Hey, you three!" yelled Coach. "Go into the dining room with the others! Chow time, then back out to work!"

The three turned their heads away, shifting their cloaks to mask their faces. They followed the others.

Lily felt terrified, being near so many guns, so many angry men.

They snaked up halls and down halls and through cloisters. They followed the rest into the dining room. Mob guards stood along the walls.

The procession of monks put down their rocks in a pile by the door and filed along the two sides of the table. Miserably they all sat at once.

Katie, Lily, and Jasper sat with them, heads bowed low. Lily folded her hands and rocked her knuckles back and forth on the table, to have something to do.

Another monk came in with a big vat of tree-squid. It was a Friday, so the monastery was serving fish. He dished out some tentacle and eyeballs for each monk. When everyone had been served, a mobster banged on a gong. They took out their wooden sporks and started eating.

The three kids were hunkered as low as they could over their bowls of squid. They didn't want anyone to see their faces—or their hair, especially. All the monks were shaved bald. This was a time when Lily really regretted her bangs. They kept flopping in front of her eyes. This was a situation when bangs might mean death. Or, as the mobsters might have put it, bangs might mean ka-pow.

Jasper was slurping up tentacle when the monk next to him (a master artist from the scriptorium) whispered, "Brother Dash. You have returned like the lark in spring."

Jasper replied, "The lark never strays too long from the nest."

"Even when the tree is charred," said the

monk sadly. "And cut down and the wood is treated and pressurized and made into an easy-to-assemble lawn gazebo."

"A cry was sent out by Brother Pghlik."

"You will not find Brother Pghlik here. He stood up to the invader, and they cut him down and locked him in the board game and tiger closet."

"With the tiger?!"

"And the board games. We fear he has been eaten." The old monk took a bite. "Stones do not weep: The water freezes on their faces."

"We've got to save him!"

"Things are very bad here, young Dash. These evil men take their children into the forbidden places in the monastery, to the flame-pits, and hold them before the sacred fires. Their children acquire magical strengths that many men study years to acquire. We seek to acquire those powers with wisdom. They acquire them with foolishness. They steal our priceless treasures and they take them away from the monastery to sell in other lands. They gather wealth so that they may be the most powerful robbers in the—"

He fell silent. His old eyes glistened as he saw the seven Stare-Eyes players walk in with Coach and Team Mom.

Jasper, Katie, and Lily felt their stomachs sink. The squid weighed heavily.

The seven players walked around the dining hall, sneering.

"Okay, girls!" roared Coach, and the monks all stopped eating and looked up at him, except three in the middle of the table, who kept looking down.

Coach smiled and crossed his arms. "We just got back from a little trip. A little trip to other states. Outside Delaware."

Team Mom snarled, "Our fingers are strong from clawing our way to the top."

Her husband said, "We sold over two million smackers' worth of your monastery garbage to museums. Statues and cups and stuff. Bye-bye. You ain't going to see it no more."

"No more," said Team Mom.

"Now. We need a little help," said Coach. "Because tonight we want to soup up the kids. Give them some more magic power. Already, they can hypnotize by looking. That worked out real well for them. We can do some brain-talking. That's great. But we want them levitating by a week from now."

"Floating," said Team Mom.

"In the air. Magically. You savvy?" Coach made a whistling, rising-up noise and made two of his fingers float like legs over his other hand. "Now we know it's not just putting the kids in front of the sacred flames. They also got to hear the right stuff to think about. And we wonder which one of you clowns is going to tell us."

"You only give us what we'll take anyway," said Team Mom. "We take the best for our chupperkins." She rubbed the blond head of the nearest team member fondly. "They are our best boys. They deserve everything wonderful."

There was a silence in the dining hall. No one wanted to help the Stare-Eyes team levitate.

They were awful enough already. Who wanted them to be awful in windows and on roofs?

"Who's going to spill the beans?" said Coach. "Who's going to tell them how to levitate?"

No one raised their hand. The Stare-Eyes Champs walked back and forth along the length of the table.

And then #6 stopped just opposite Jasper. He turned his head to the side.

And he said, "Hey! Look here!" He pointed. Jasper had been recognized.

57

#6 froze. His mouth was open. His finger was raised. He didn't move. Jasper held his gaze furiously.

Their eyes were locked. Invisibly, their spirits struggled like sumo wrestlers bulging with the flab of anger.

Everyone stared. #6 still pointed into empty space.

"Oh, me?" said the monk next to Jasper. "The young gentleman points to me? Yes, I will tell all. The sea cannot hold back its tides when the moon calls." He rose up. "It is decided, then. I will tell you the secrets of levitation. You will hold these excellent children before the sacred flames."

"Great," said Coach.

"But you must know, there is great danger in

being broasted in the flame-pits of Vbngoom if you have not had the proper training."

"So how long will the proper training take? We can get a whiteboard up here, some Magic Markers. What kind of time do you need?"

"Twenty-five years, thirty years," said the monk. "Then they shall be ready to face the flames."

"No go," said the Coach. "Why don't we try to get them levitating by four-thirty tomorrow? That's what I call thinking like a winner."

The monk frowned. "You endanger your children," he said.

"You say no, and we'll hang some of the littler monks out the window by their heels again."

The monk sighed. "Then by tomorrow," he said.

"See? Attitude improvement. Rah rah rah. Stars and stripes in the air. Let's go." Coach snapped. "Come with us."

"I leave my squid behind me," said the old man, nodding. "So shall we all, on our last day, abandon our squid."

#6 trembled. He wanted to yell out. Every-thing in him tried to sound a warning. But he was locked in place by Jasper's glare.

Behind them, the other boys filed out of the room, giving each other the high five. Coach and Team Mom led the way, with the old monk between them.

#6 remained behind.

For many minutes, his eyes and Jasper's stayed locked.

The other monks left. The gangsters left. Still, Jasper, Katie, and Lily sat at the table, and #6 stood, pointing, his eyes glazed, his mouth open.

Twenty minutes later, Jasper unhooked his gaze, wiped his mouth on his napkin, and said, "Jakeloo. And we're off."

They left. #6 remained standing, hypnotized.

Later that evening, someone was thoughtful enough to rest a bowl of after-dinner mints on #6's outstretched hand. They hung a sign from his arm that read, HOWDY! ASK US ABOUT OUR HOMEMADE SPINACH QUICHE!

They were really good mints.

58

As soon as they had left the dining room, Jasper led them away from the other monks. "We've got to go unlock the board game and tiger closet," he said. "That's where they're keeping Drgnan Pghlik."

They walked carefully through the monastery, up hallways and stairs.

Lily was amazed by what she saw. She loved how ancient and mysterious everything was. She felt a thrill when she saw the old paintings on the walls, obscured by years of smoke: pictures of the beginning of the world or its end, the cracking of the globe; acts of heroism and generosity from previous ages played out in crowns of gold and coats of satin on mountaintops and forests.

There were paintings of the huts of hermits and the courts of kings.

She wanted to spend a lifetime learning about them, about all of their secret meanings. Why did one saint bake bread made of sand, while another was covered with grasshoppers? Each picture had its secret story. As they rushed past them, Lily wanted to pause and study them all.

But there was no time.

Carefully Jasper led them up a final twisting staircase. The door at the top was latched. Slowly he drew up the latch and pressed with his fingertips so the door swung inward.

It was a recreation room. There was a Ping-Pong table, as well as stacks of other entertainments: a toboggan, the monastery's water-polo net, a croquet set, and so on. At the far end of the room was a closet door with a key in the keyhole. A sound of growling, like a wild beast with the taste of monk-flesh on its tongue, came from the closet.

A mobster guard was posted to the room. He

was asleep, curled up on the air-hockey table. He had his thumb in his mouth.

Carefully Jasper, Katie, and Lily crept across the floor. The mobster snored.

The imprisoned tiger made an answering growl.

Jasper hoped that Drgnan Pghlik was still uneaten, at least most of him.

Lily couldn't stop staring at the gangster. He had a gun. A real gun. He probably had killed people before, except he would call it "bumping them off" or "zotzing" or "croakin' 'em good."

Lily knew that you should never stare at anyone when you don't want them to see you. Even if you have never been exposed to the sacred fires of Vbngoom, there is some weird way that people can feel it when you stare at them, even if they can't see you. Lily knew this, and didn't want to alert the mobster, but she couldn't tear her eyes away because she was so frightened of him.

Meanwhile the Boy Technonaut was standing by the board game and tiger closet. He reached out and very gently turned the key in the lock.

The door swung open.

There was Drgnan Pghlik with his eyes closed. He looked completely calm, although his head was in the tiger's mouth, with the animal's fangs pressing into his cheek and neck.

The boy opened his eyes with a snap. He saw Jasper, and his face lit up with joy.

Jasper, Lily, and Katie put their fingers over their lips to shush him.

He reached out and grabbed Jasper's hand in a hearty shake. It jiggled the tiger.

Nrrrgarha, seeing the open door, let Drgnan go. Drgnan sprang out of the closet. Jasper stepped into the closet, over the tiger, and scanned the games quickly.

Drgnan looked at him quizzically. Jasper held up the ray gun for Drgnan to see, and opened its battery compartment. Drgnan nodded, checked to see that the ray gun required triple-A batteries, and then pulled out a toy robot from the stack of games.

Jasper turned the robot over to find the battery pack. Its eyes lit up. In a loud recorded voice like a gravel-grinder, it bellowed, *"Have no fear! Gau-Grza to the Rescue!"*

And with that, the gangster sat up.

59

"Whoa! Kid with a dress is sprung!" said the gangster, and raised his gun.

Lily ducked—

—which would not have saved her from flying bullets—

—but did save her from being whacked by the monastery tiger leaping through the air and onto the gangster.

The gangster was knocked backward. His gun fell to the floor. Lily, Katie, Jasper, and Drgnan backed away, appalled. The gangster and the tiger wrestled on the air-hockey table.

I would hate to have to report that the tiger ate the gangster, even if the gangster was a very bad person.

So let's jump three minutes ahead.

Plans! Plans! Jasper and Lily ran one way, to try to warn the other monks that an uprising was afoot. Katie and Drgnan Pghlik ran the other way to try to stop the Stare-Eyes team from gaining secret powers from the sacred flame deep in the catacombs beneath the monastery.

The tiger went his own way, looking for more gangster meat.

Through the temple Katie and Drgnan sprinted, pillars fluttering past as they dashed. On all of the pedestals were dark places where statues of gold and silver had stood—statues now dragged away and sold to make money for the World-Wide Lootery. Drgnan reached a huge stone ogre and pressed a series of warts. A secret door slid open.

Meanwhile Lily and Jasper took steps two by two. They ran up toward the dormitories. Jasper slid the batteries from the robot into his gun. He snapped the grip shut. Jasper and Lily scampered across a landing.

Bullets! Mobsters fired!

Jasper and Lily crouched at the turn in the stairs. Jasper shot bolts of light from his ray gun—there was an angry curse from above—and he and Lily smelled the scent of burning polyester. He had hit one of the mobsters smack in the cheap suit.

Katie and Drgnan now rushed through halls buried deep within the mountain. Candles and torches lit the way.

"Where are the sacred flames?" asked Katie.

"In the heart of the mountain," said Drgnan Pghlik. "They are the source of all our power. These Stare-Eyes children and their mobster parents do not understand the power of the flames. There is much danger there."

There was much danger everywhere.

60

Jasper was locked in a gun battle with the mob. He fired his laser.

Lily hated gunplay. She didn't think violence was a good idea. She always hoped it could be avoided through the use of false mustaches, clever ploys, logical conversation, and a few rolling boulders.

But Jasper was desperately blasting away at the enemy. Lily felt like she couldn't just stand there and do nothing while he protected her. Especially because, as usual, his batteries weren't going to last forever. She'd noticed his gun went through batteries kind of quickly. Pretty soon, his laser beam was going to get all dim and fizzly.

Bullets zinged past her. She closed her eyes, trembling.

Jasper fired. There was another curse word down the corridor, and Weasel Chops O'Reilly said, "He almost fried my kisser! You little punk! I'm gonna need that some day! For kissing!"

"I hope not, you scoundrel!" said Jasper. "I hope that no woman ever calls the number on the clammy little scraps of paper you doubtless force into their hands at hamburger rallies and 4-H fairs!"

Jasper did not have a very clear idea of where gangsters met their ladies. Weasel Chops O'Reilly usually met his classy dames down at the booze joints on the corner of Squat Street and Hard Luck or at prizefights between battling robots.

Meanwhile Lily didn't know what to do.

"Lily," said Jasper. "I'll hold off the gangsters. You run down that hallway there to the dormitories! Tell the monks what's happening! Ask them where I can find Bobby Spandrel!"

Lily nodded and ran down the hallway.

Jasper fired around the corner at the mobsters. His forehead had broken out into a sweat.

Lily ran as fast as she could to the door of the monks' dormitories. "Hurry!" yelled Jasper behind her. "I can't hold them for long!" Lily hurried. She threw the door open to find the monks all kneeling on the floor, serenely praying.

"Um," she said, "um, excuse me."

The monks looked up.

Lisa Buldene was sitting there, too, trying to work her cell phone. She looked up in astonishment. "It's the girl from Dover! How did you get in?"

"Never mind, Ms. Buldene! We've got to get out!" To the monks, she said, "Jasper Dash—he was here years ago, you might remember him— anyway, Jasper Dash is holding the gangsters off!"

There were happy nods when they heard that Jasper Dash had returned.

"Jasper needs help finding Bobby Spandrel, the leader of the gang!"

This is normally the place in the story when the monks would all agree to help fight the mobsters, and everyone would cheer and rush out of the room and victory would follow immediately.

Unfortunately, these monks had taken a vow of complete nonviolence, so biffing gangsters in the schnozz was out of the question. Their martial arts training was not supposed to actually be used for fighting, but instead as a way of exercising the mind and combating the inner demons such as anger, desire for worldly goods, and procrastination. Not stooges with machine guns.

Oh, yeah, the machine guns. There was a lot of gunfire coming from the staircase now.

Lily felt very nervous.

But let's change the scene.

Deep beneath the earth, Katie and Drgnan Pghlik raced through the catacombs. They lifted their knees high and scampered past tombs guarded by serpents. They slid down the banister of the crematorium.

Drgnan Pghlik threw open a bronze door.

They stepped into a huge cavern. It was lit by a weird, flickering blue light. Some daylight came from above. The cave had once been part of a volcano, and there was a hole that led straight up and out the top of the mountain.

But the eerie blue light came from below. There was a huge chasm in the middle of the floor, a fissure, a crack. It divided the room into two. And deep down there in the heart of the mountain was a blue glow: the sacred flames. Gases rose from the depths and wafted up into the rock chimney above.

Suspended above the chasm and the flame were five of the players from the Stare-Eyes team.

The boys hung from the ceiling. They sat cradled in chains, with their arms folded, their legs crossed, and their eyes open. The chain baskets dangled them over the pit so they could soak up the energies radiating from the mountain's heart.

Their eyes glowed red, and their pupils were slits like snakes'.

They bathed in the light from the flame-pits of Delaware.

61

The dangling varsity players were in a trance. They did not move or seem to see. They just sat with folded arms and legs crossed, staring into space.

Drgnan Pghlik counted. "That's not all of them, is it?" he asked Katie.

"No," said Katie. "We caught their Number Four in Dover. And Number Six is frozen upstairs in the dining room." She scanned their faces. "And Number One is missing."

"See!" said Drgnan. "There is their coach!"

Katie looked across the chasm. There on the other side of the cavern was Coach, leaning against the wall, grinning, and drinking, as he would say, "a brewski." He stood next to a large lever attached to some sort of machine.

"What's that machine?" Katie asked Drgnan.

"It is a lever that controls the chains that hold people over the flame-pits. The chains are on a track in the ceiling. The lever, yes? It draws the chains over to that side of the chasm so that people can step off and the holy do not dangle forever."

Katie inspected the room carefully. She looked up at the hanging jocks, at the mechanical track that held them in place, and at Coach, sitting by the engine that would move them. She saw that a bridge, also made of chains, ran across the fissure, right under the five meditating mob kids.

"I have an idea," she said. "We can trap those five."

Drgnan squinted. "What does my clever sister mean?"

"If we break that machine or pull out a gear or something, then the five players will be stuck there, you know, at our mercy. They won't be able to escape."

"Ah!" Drgnan exclaimed with pleasure. "Indeed! The lever on this machine unscrews!"

"Okay," said Katie. "If you can take on Coach, I can take care of the lever."

Drgnan smiled. "It is an excellent plan," he said. "So we cross the bridge."

Katie inspected the glinting bridge. It swayed with gusts of blue that drifted up from the mystical flames beneath.

Katie's palms were sweating. She wasn't sure how excellent a plan it was, suddenly.

She and Drgnan started to creep across the cavern floor.

They were almost at the chain bridge beneath the dandled, zombie-eyed boys—when Coach saw them.

"Hey! Hey!" Coach belted. "You! Keep away from my boys! They're winners, and you're a bad influence!"

The coach ran forward and pulled his pistol out of his tracksuit.

Katie and Drgnan dropped to the floor behind an outcropping. Flights of bullets rattled against the stalagmites, the stalactites, the schist.

Katie whispered to Drgnan, "Okay. How are we going to do this?"

"Saint Lrtzmrk writes that when the falcon lands in the lagoon, then the frog seeks its dinner elsewhere," said Drgnan.

"You don't have the faintest idea, do you?"

"No, my sister. None whatsoever."

Katie peeked up over her outcropping—at the pit, at their adversary, at the five boys dreaming in the radiance of the sacred flames below them.

More bullets flew by.

And then Katie realized: Some of those bullets were coming from behind them.

She turned and grunted in surprise.

#1 stood in the door behind them, firing at their backs.

They were trapped.

62

Lily and Jasper were in a corridor full of monks. There was a lot of monastic excitement in the air. The monks conferred. They agreed: They had to get outside to safety, beyond the reach of the mob.

As they went down the hall, Jasper asked one of the older monks, "Your Holiness, are you sure you don't know the whereabouts of Bobby Spandrel? The leader of the gang? Just a little taller than me? Round, silver, featureless head? No hands or feet?"

"All of the gangsters have had faces," answered the monk. "Except inside their hearts. There they have no faces whatsoever."

"This way," one of the monks ordered.

Jasper nodded. "We'll get everyone out of

the monastery, and then I'll slip back in to look for that villain Spandrel."

They all hurried along the passageway toward the exit. Lisa Buldene was snapping pictures as fast as she could. "This is amazing!" she said. "I'm almost being shot at! Now I'm really alive!"

The passage came out at a flight of steps that led down the side of the volcanic crater to a little bridge. The monks poured down the steps.

And stopped.

There were ten gangsters in one big clump in front of them. Waiting.

The monks poured back up the steps.

"Secret door! Secret door!" they said, giddy with motion. Lily, Jasper, Lisa Buldene, and the monks scurried down a hall to a domed, circular chapter house. One slid a lectern aside and pointed at a secret passageway that led down.

They all ran down the cramped staircase—a hundred monks or more. They came out in a courtyard. They started to run for the exit.

And then saw, coming to block them, the same parade of ten toughs.

So the group ran back through the secret door, up the steps, out of the domed chapter house, down the hallway, and tried a bridge.

But now the mobsters were on the other side of the bridge, waiting for them.

So the group turned and ran back.

"To the spoons! To the spoons!" the monks called. They charged up stairs and arrived on the roof of a tower. There was one of the vault-apults there, with a trigger to pull it back and release it.

"Two by two!" a monk called. "We will be shot over the gangsters' heads to that tower, where we shall make our way . . ."

The words died on his lips. He was pointing at another tower, but mobsters poured out of a trapdoor there and stood, arms folded, waiting to receive whoever landed there.

Lily looked at the other towers.

Mobsters. Mobsters. Mobsters.

"Pyramids of Snefru!" Jasper swore. "We're trapped, chaps!"

"It's like they knew where we were going!" said Lily.

"It's like someone was . . ." Jasper stopped talking.

"Like someone was what?" said Lisa Buldene.

Jasper looked down. "Like someone was *telling* the gangsters which direction we were going in all the time."

"Who would do a rotten thing like that?" said Lisa Buldene.

Full of rage, Jasper looked her in the eye. He said, "I should have known—the moment I saw your pants."

"My pants?"

"No human being would willingly wear pants that zipped off at the knee—no normal human being—unless *they had rocket-thrusters in place of their detachable feet.*"

Lily stared aghast at the New Yorker. Could it be?

Lisa Buldene's hand was on her own throat. Her fingers were plucking at her skin. . . . *Scrabble, scrabble, scrabble* . . . Pulling on her chin . . . *Yanking off her face!*

Her real head was a foot-and-a-half-wide silver sphere that rang with energy and static. She cast off her rubber hands.

"Bobby Spandrel," said Jasper, with disgust.

"We meet again, Boy Technonaut," said the international arch-criminal. "But this, I believe, will be the last time."

63

Katie Mulligan and Drgnan Pghlik crouched in the cavern by the flame-pits, fired on from both sides. In front of them, across the pit, was Coach. Behind them, near the door, was #1.

Bullets splintered stone. Drgnan squatted flat and clucked with his tongue.

Suddenly Katie had another idea.

Over the din of lead, she shouted, "We need to get near the boys! No one will shoot us if we're near the—"

No time to explain—she grabbed Drgnan Pghlik's hand and tugged. Together they rushed forward, toward the edge of the pit, toward the bridge—and the Coach rushed toward them. He stood on the opposite cliff, taking aim.

The girl and the monk had reached the chasm. They faced the enemy.

Coach stood at the other end of the bridge. He trained his pistol.

And suddenly Drgnan Pghlik jumped, hurled himself into the air, and grabbed at the first chained, meditating kid. With both hands, he clamped on, and that first jock rocked—slamming into the next one—

Coach frowned.

The second jock knocked the third, the third jock knocked the fourth, the fourth jock knocked the fifth—and Coach, on the opposite cliff, was whacked sprawling. He stumbled—arms up—and fell off the edge of the cliff. He tumbled about eight feet to another little cliff, where he lodged, knocked out, spread-eagled, almost upside down.

Katie, wobbling, crossed the bridge. It swayed. It bucked. It heaved like a dog spitting up.

#1 had run to the chasm behind them,

jumped, and now hung from another one of his team members, kicking and punching at Drgnan. Drgnan defended with knees and wrist blocks. The team, suspended, rocked back and forth, slamming into one another. Drgnan and #1 threw themselves from side to side to avoid getting crushed between meditating sport-brats. They hurled punches around the arms of the glow-eyed boys.

Katie stepped off the bridge and ran to grab the lever. If she could unscrew that lever, the boys would be trapped in their chain cages. Even if they woke up from their trances, they couldn't free themselves. She made a dash for the controls to the sacred rotisserie.

She grabbed the lever. She didn't know how to detach it. She struggled with it. She pulled it to one side.

Suddenly an engine cranked to life, and the five suspended boys—and Drgnan and #1, holding fast, flailing—began trundling toward her.

If they reached her side of the cliff, Katie

realized, and somehow woke up, then suddenly there would be six people to fight instead of just one. But if she didn't get the baskets to safe ground, then Drgnan Pghlik would be trapped hanging on to them above the abyss.

Drgnan and #1 struggled on the swaying champs. #1 hissed to the monk, "I've eaten bigger animals than you." He showed his teeth. His eyes were green slits. He lashed out with a kick that sent his champ into a spin and caught Drgnan on the side of the head.

Drgnan almost lost his grip. He grabbed for the chains.

Katie threw the lever the other way. The machinery clanked and reversed. The line of athletes started rolling back out over the pit.

"Fortune smiles, my sister!" yelled Drgnan Pghlik. He blocked a punch to his gut. He called to her, "Unscrew the lever!"

"You'll be trapped!"

"Quickly!" said Drgnan.

The athletes were hanging above the center of

the flame-pits again. There they stopped. Katie began unscrewing the lever.

It was free—she had it—and she ran back to the bridge.

She looked at Drgnan fighting valiantly. She thought that the two of them made a good team. Her and him. Fighting crime, side by side. She was suddenly electric with joy in adventure.

At last Coach was sitting up, looking around. His gun had fallen into the flame-pit.

Katie rushed over him, clambering across the bridge of chains. Drgnan and #1 popped up and down around the swaying teammates. Drgnan looked battered, hanging awkwardly by one hand and one foot, his robe torn, his head reeling.

Katie began swatting at #1 from below with the lever, as if he were a particularly obnoxious piñata.

#1 growled.

A hand—#1 swooped his hand down from above and grabbed Katie's arm. She roared in protest. She slapped him. Grunting, he lifted her.

Her wrist burned with his grip, but it was all that kept her from falling into the blue flames. She looked down at the tangled energies of the mountain, the loops and licks of magical fire that roiled below.

Her arm creaked and popped. She hung, slowly sliding out of #1's grip.

"Say good-bye," said #1.

She felt his fingers loosen their hold on her wrist.

She fell.

Drgnan swung—he let go—he dropped.

She tumbled.

The flames grew brighter—rocks flashed past.

Drgnan grabbed her. His arm was wrapped around her.

And suddenly she wasn't falling.

They were deep down in the throat of the mountain, hanging in midair.

"You levitate," she said, looking into his eyes. His arm was very strong.

"The mind is as still as a concrete pool," he said.

And with that, they floated upward. Past the suspended team members who hung there helpless, basted in magic. Past #1, who was trapped, holding on to one of the chains, unable to get to either cliff.

Katie, with her arm around Drnan Pghlik and his arm around her, was shooting up toward the light of day.

64

Jasper Dash and Bobby Spandrel faced each other on the tower top. From the chimneys below, the scent of burning fir boughs and candle wax was carried on the breeze across the mountain peaks.

"Bobby Spandrel, you scoundrel," said Jasper. "You have disturbed all these good people just to get your revenge on me."

"I am tired of you," said Bobby Spandrel in his awful, tinny, electronic voice. "I try to just carry out a simple, straightforward plan where I levitate the Egyptian Sphinx so I can fly over the sea and rob banks in Rio de Janeiro, and you're there with a cable to trip me up. I try to counterfeit the Canadian dollar in the basement of a haunted house, and you kick open the secret door and foil my designs. I try to set up a blorgassium smuggling ring on the planet Neptune, and you're there crawling through the air ducts. I am tired of you, Jasper Dash. I hate you. So this is the end, my flustered friend. You will never bother me again."

"You monster!" said Jasper. "Why didn't you finish me off when you met us disguised as Lisa Buldene in Dover?"

"Because I wanted you to meet your death here, in total defeat, with the place you love most crushed beneath my thumb." He gestured with his cuffs to his hands, which lay on the floor. "I put on that woman suit so I could be assured you were on your way to this monastery, and that you knew how to get here despite the mountains shifting when it's misty. I knew you would eventually see the Vbngoom artifacts in the Pelt Museum, and I knew that if I could slip you directions, it would only be a matter of time before you sought out the monastery and were here quivering at my very feet." He gestured at the fake feet at the ends of his zip-off pants. "So now you're here. And now you're gone. That's it. It's time to bash Jasper Dash." He called shrilly, "Men!"

From the staircase, several toughs appeared. Team Mom was among them.

"And woman," said Team Mom. "I'm here, too."

"Men and woman! Throw him over the parapet!" Bobby Spandrel ordered. "Make sure he makes a squishy sound at the bottom."

They walked toward Jasper.

But they couldn't get to him.

The monks all moved in and stood in the way. They crossed their arms.

And right in front of Jasper stood Lily, looking defiant and nervous.

"We won't let you hurt our friend," said the monk in front.

The mobsters stopped inches from the monks. More monks moved up and confronted them.

"You will never learn," said Jasper to his enemy, "that friendship is stronger than hate."

Bobby Spandrel didn't laugh, because that wasn't the kind of thing they did with their lungs where he came from. But he *seemed* to laugh, and he said, "And you, Boy Technonaut, will never learn: It's not much good to have your fighting done by friends who have sworn an oath of nonviolence." Spandrel swung his empty sleeve in a broad gesture. He ordered his goons, "Push right through the monks."

"Move out of the way, baldy," growled Team Mom. "There are events that need to happen."

Bobby Spandrel taunted the monks, "You pledged to never attack anyone. You can't do anything. So move out of her way."

The monk in front said, "We also pledged to protect our guests and our friends. We will use nonviolence to help them."

"Ignore him!" cried Bobby Spandrel. "Grab Jasper Dash—and *smash smash smash*."

The gangsters—Team Mom among them—

reared back and plunged into the crowd of monks—

Or would have if the monks hadn't stood their ground. They didn't move. The gangsters raised their hands to push the monks out of the way. And then a most extraordinary fight broke out. Monks vs. gangsters.

The way life should be.

Of course, it's a little difficult to describe this fight, since half of the people fighting couldn't in fact, um, fight, but it went down somewhat like this:

Weasel Chops O'Reilly goes to smack a monk on the head—raises his hand—and the monk blocks his blow with a sincere hope for universal friendship and kindness! Weasel Chops tries a left-hand hook to the jaw, but the monk counters with a wish that all men and women could coexist peacefully, living in geodesic domes! Gurgling with fury, Weasel Chops throws a quick right to the monk's face—but just before his punch connects, the monk whaps him on the back of the head with a vision of an elk in a sunlit clearing standing next to its young! Weasel Chops goes reeling, clutching his skull!

Team Mom seizes a monk's green robe and hauls him to the side! She elbows another monk in the gut! She grabs his neck! He flails for a second and then delivers a swift, powerful plea for world peace to the nose! She stumbles backward and grabs at his arm, twists as she falls. He fights back with a recipe for unleavened bread! She hits him in the chin; he gasps and pummels her with the thought of calico kittens riding on the back of a friendly shark!

She throws him to the side! But he's not so easily defeated: He is *a master of haiku*! She delivers a roundhouse kick to the stomach. And he? He uses the power of poetry! Like:

We could sip dark wine.
Best friends go eat layer cake.
Ow. You bit my arm.

And:

The lake reflects sky.
So do our eyes show the soul.
Your left one is black.

Bobby Spandrel, his round head buzzing with irritation, saw Team Mom get a black eye from poetry—he saw his mobsters being walloped by a bunch of monks, and he was furious.

He raised his empty sleeve and blasted a huge bolt of energy in Jasper's direction.

Lily threw herself to the ground just in time. Everyone screamed and ducked—they kept writhing on the ground, wrestling, saying, "Oof!"

Jasper and Bobby Spandrel faced each other again over all the wriggling bodies.

Jasper climbed into the vaultapult. He fired his ray gun at Spandrel, but another burst of energy from Bobby's arm blocked the beam.

Bobby took aim and fired right at the Boy Technonaut.

And at the exact same moment, Jasper fired himself into the air from the vaultapult.

He soared up into the sky above the monastery. The energy bolt flew harmlessly past his feet. It shuttled along through the mountain passes. Jasper spun in the clear blue.

Roaring with anger, Bobby Spandrel launched himself into the air, blowing off his fake rubber feet as his ankles ignited with jets.

Seeing that Jasper was airborne, two gangsters from other towers launched themselves to intercept him and beat him up in midair.

Lily rose to her feet unsteadily and watched as Jasper twirled over the volcanic crater and prepared to meet the two toughs winging their way toward him. She held her breath.

A gangster flew up, passed Jasper, and got socked in the jaw—POW!—and, dizzy-eyed, fell.

Bobby Spandrel flew toward Jasper as Jasper hurtled toward a far trampoline. Jasper spun, firing off several shots from his ray gun at Bobby before he hit the taut oxhide and was hurled back up into the air, wheeling his legs in kicks and punches to knock out the gangsters who grabbed at his knees.

Now more monks shouldered past Lily and crawled into the vaultapult to throw themselves toward Jasper so they could help. Lily felt useless. She didn't know what to do. Most of the gangsters on her tower were out of commission—so worn down and humbled by the monks' superior powers of love and gentleness that they couldn't even stand up anymore. They just sat around weeping, thinking about how long it had been since they'd played with their dogs and visited their great-aunts at the nursing home. Team Mom was completely knocked out.

Lily watched, astonished, as gangsters from the far towers shot themselves toward the monks to beat them up in midair.

Meanwhile Bobby Spandrel had swooped down and grabbed the bouncing Jasper in his stumpy arms. Jasper beat on his archenemy's metal limbs. It made a sound like an angry person cooking. *Whang, whang, whang!*

Bobby Spandrel blasted back up over the volcanic crater.

Far below his feet, which kicked helplessly in midair, Jasper saw the weird blue light from the flame-pits of Vbngoom. He wished—dearly wished—he'd brought his jetpack. It did not always work well—it had often sent him spiraling into sugar maples—but he was, he figured, looking at certain death without it. When Bobby Spandrel dropped him, which was going to happen close to immediately, Jasper would fall hundreds of feet into the maw of blue fire.

"Good-bye, Boy Technonaut."

Jasper decided to spend a brief moment thinking of all the things he loved in life. Of course, he thought of his mother, who turned from the oven to smile one last smile at him. He thought of s'mores, when the chocolate was still firm but the marshmallow was gooey. He thought of bike rides in the autumn, when the leaves tangle in your hair. He thought of the simple pleasures of excavating a burial chamber booby-trapped with spikes and pythons.

And he thought of Lily, standing below him

somewhere—brave, stolid, quiet Lily, always generous, always thinking about others and what beat in their hearts—Lily, who would have to watch him drop to his death.

And Katie. If only Katie could be there—fun, funny, kind of obnoxious Katie with her gruff jokes and her golden smile. He was glad he had enjoyed the friendship of these two, which had made the last few—

Yeah, okay. Stop the violins.

Because Bobby Spandrel has just dropped Jasper feetfirst into the flame-pits of Delaware.

65

Jasper Dash, Boy Technonaut, plummeted to certain doom.

Bobby Spandrel
hovered.

Monks flew out over the abyss
in rebounding volleys
and lofted through the blue,

$SPUN,$ and met

Lily saw Jasper falling.
Her heart felt like it was dying.
She screamed.

JASPER FELL.

Here's Nrrrgarha, the monastery

t i g e r !

Gangsters flew out over the abyss
in rebounding volleys.
One held his breath because
he thought it was
like diving.
And with a CRASH they met
their enemies midair!

AND SHOOTING UP THROUGH THE MIDDLE OF IT ALL WAS...

66

Drgnan Pghlik and Katie!

They had levitated up out of the volcanic chimney, and now passed Jasper—saw him—screeched to a halt—dropped—and grabbed him, too.

"Drgnan," said Jasper, "I am happier to see you than a new copper penny."

"Gosh," said Katie, looking around her. Monks were flying through the air, their robes rippling. Gangsters were hurled through space, arms and legs straight at their sides, the pinstripes on their suits like zoom-lines in a cartoon. "What's going on here?"

Then the blasts of energy started whizzing past, fired from Bobby Spandrel's missing hands.

Jasper fired his laser back up.

"I cannot hold you both for long," said Drgnan Pghlik. "Away from the flames, my power weakens."

"Look out!" said Jasper. "That scourge Spandrel is coming to engage us in fisticuffs! Prepare for a set-to, chums!"

Lily, helpless below, watched as Bobby Spandrel descended on the three hovering kids. He fired his photon blasters, and Jasper deflected with his ray gun, and then suddenly they were all tangled up in a big bunch, flailing and whomping at Spandrel's robotic limbs.

Lily detected a movement to her right. It was Team Mom, rising, her eye swollen shut from the fierce blows of haiku. Mom pulled her pistol out of the waistband of her tracksuit and pointed it up at Drgnan, Jasper, and Katie.

Lily quietly put her foot out and tripped her.

Team Mom fell sprawling on the stones. Monks stepped gingerly across her to reach the vaultapult. They were still firing themselves into the air. At this point, most of the gangsters were defeated. Lily started to suspect that the monks just liked flying.

Now many of them who knew how to levitate were hovering around the fierce boxing match being fought in the sky between Dash, Mulligan, Pghlik, and Spandrel. The monks were in ranks and rows, floating in the clouds, watching, like a Renaissance painting of someone going to Heaven.

The three kids had seized on Bobby Spandrel's robotic arms and his robotic legs. They wouldn't let go. Bobby Spandrel couldn't shoot them, because they had control of his arms, and he couldn't shake them off.

"Let go!" he demanded. "Let go, so I can blow you to oblivion!"

"Nothing doing, you villain!" cried Jasper. "You might as well give up now. We've got you, Spandrel, like a dog and his master's sock!"

Bobby Spandrel fought—struggled— groaned—growled—shrugged—kicked—found himself pinned—

And so he detached his head.

Bobby Spandrel's body with the three kids still attached shot downward.

But his head stayed stuck on the blue sky.

"Farewell, Dash, and fall well! I flee to fight another day! Away!"

And with that, the silver globe bobbed upward, shot through the ranks of floating monks, and hurtled toward the moon.

Meanwhile, the three kids and Bobby Spandrel's empty body were caught by levitating monks. They were brought gently back to earth.

Everything was confusion. There were collapsed gangsters everywhere and monks in the air. There were monks on trampolines, their robes swishing around their legs. They looked like they were having a lot of fun.

The score, in case you've forgotten—I have—is like this:

Gangsters: Beaten by the power of meekness, humility, and generosity.

Team Mom: Knocked out by poetry and Lily.

Coach: Stranded on a little cliff down in the volcano.

Stare-Eyes Team #4: In the hospital in Dover.

Stare-Eyes Team #2, 3, 5, 7, 8: Hanging in baskets over the flame-pits.

Stare-Eyes Team #1: Hanging on to #5, who is hanging over the flame-pits.

Stare-Eyes Team #6: Being used as an announcement board and a dispenser for after-dinner mints.

Bobby Spandrel: Lost body. Head escapes to fight another day, ha ha!

Monks: Full of joy and leaping.

And I think that should about do it. That's everyone. That's a wrap.

The battle was over. The monks had won.

67

That night there was a great feast in the monastery of Vbngoom, the Platter of Heaven.

Everyone got an extra plate of oak leaves and acorns. Lily, Katie, and Jasper got lentil stew—without sleeping potion.

Torches were lit on all the walls, and the few lightbulbs they had were switched on to celebrate their victory.

Now they could send monks out into the world to reclaim their statues and artifacts. They had lists of all the museums that had bought their stolen treasures. Some of the repo monks would be going to Pelt, to reclaim the three objects purchased illegally by Mr. Lecroix. They said they would take Lily, Katie, and Jasper back with them, since Jasper's flying Gyroscopic Sky Suite was defunct.

The four friends—Katie, Jasper, Lily, and now Drgnan—stood on the walls of the monastery, looking out over the mountains. There were forests below them, and more distantly, fields, and the hazy lights of Wilmington to the north. Sky and earth were the color of powder. Jungles were a black, grizzled line. Darkness was falling.

"The day after tomorrow," said Katie, "we'll be home. Soft beds. Hamburgers. Showers that don't have a goat in them."

"There is not a goat in the shower here," said Drgnan Pghlik, a little hurt. "That is an alpaca."

"No," said Katie, patting him on the wrist. "I'm talking about our hotel. It was a goat there."

Suddenly Lily announced, "I don't want to go back." She looked longingly at a statue of a many-armed hero on a kind of granite unicycle. A little embarrassed, she explained, "I just . . . I want to stay here and study all the ancient legends." Now that she had said it, she felt silly, like Lisa Buldene, loving everything Delawarian—

everything—with a starry-eyed adoration. If Lisa Buldene hadn't turned out to be an eyeless, handless, footless interdimensional criminal.

"Don't you want to see your mom and dad again?" Katie asked.

"Sure," said Lily quietly. "Of course, yeah. But I've never been anyplace like this before."

Jasper solemnly said, "It's a place like no other." He admitted, "There are times, chaps, when back at home, I almost feel out of step with the present day. When I notice that the other lads on the Pelt Stare-Eyes team, for example, think I'm somehow . . ." He couldn't find the word. No one else wanted to say anything. Finally he said, "Quaint. Old-time. Despite the fact that I am clearly perched on the leading edge of future epochs, riding the ailerons of an age when man shall even fly to distant stars." He gripped the parapet and said, "I know, Lily, Katie, that people laugh at me. I know sometimes behind my back, when I introduce my jetpack or my portable phone—"

"It was a great phone, Jasper," said Katie. "Just a little big, based on what people are used to these days. I mean, on wheels and all. With the speaking trumpet. And hard to get up steps."

"My point is that at home, I am the butt of jokes." He shook his head sadly. "See, I just said, 'butt.' I shall never learn. At home, that would earn me the titters of the team. But here, no one laughs at me. Here, people think about life and death, and good and evil, and right and wrong. Here I feel more at home than in my home. And yet, I don't belong here, either." He looked at Lily. "We don't belong."

She frowned and nodded. She blew her hair out of her eyes.

Jasper said, "You can come back anytime you want, though, and visit."

"I don't know about that," said Lily. "You, um, you kind of made a special Delaware for us somehow. I'm not sure that Katie or I could find our way back to this one alone. I'm not sure it would be here."

Katie said, "You might find less temples and brachiosauruses, and more hair parlors and J. P.

Bennigan's American Family Restaurants. And Laundromats. And the Halt'n'Buy." She smiled at Jasper. "You have to realize, you find places that most people can't find. That's one thing that's so great about you."

"Then we can all come back," said Jasper. "I shall bring you back. And Lily, you can study the statues and the paintings. Katie, you can learn martial arts. Drgnan, I will challenge you to Scrabble."

Drgnan Pghlik had watched this whole discussion with interest, but it was very foreign to him. He had not seen his true home since he was very small, when his village had been destroyed by a horde of barbarian gnomes seven or eight inches high, armed with teeny tiny little spears and itsy-bitsy broadswords. To him, therefore, Vbngoom would always be home, and he dreamed of going someday to see other American towns, like Pelt.

The four of them heard a deep, resounding moo. It was the ceremonial horns—horns so long that they required one person to blow on them and two people farther along to support them on brackets atop their hats.

The notes from the horns rang out across the hidden valley, the peaks. They rang out loud and strong. They were filled with assurance that all was well in Vbngoom and that the next day would be just like this day, and yet would bring new things.

Below, in one of the courtyards, the monks were gathering for their rites of celebration. They murmured to one another, dressed in elaborate silken robes and complicated headgear. Behind them, the blue light from the flame-pits shone up from the crater and danced on the stone walls.

Jasper and Lily strolled over to watch the monks in their ceremony. Drgnan and Katie stayed where they were, looking out at the shining water that guarded New Castle County from the realm of New Jersey. Almost nothing could be seen now of hillock, vale, or Hackensack.

"You saved my life," said Katie.

Drgnan shrugged. "When a stone drops, the ground catches it. And when the dirt falls, it lands on stone."

"Yeah, but you're a lot nicer than dirt."

"And you saved my life, too." Drgnan smiled. "You should not miss seeing the dancing ceremony," he said. "When we monks of Vbngoom dance, after a while, we levitate and float out over the valley. It is a very good sight."

Katie smiled back at him. She said, "You know, I'm going to be kind of sorry to leave too."

"It is strange," said Drgnan Pghlik. "To you, the way we live here is unusual. You are interested by our tiger and our floating. To me, the town of Pelt, which Jasper has told me of, is interesting. I have never bowled. I have never water-skied."

Katie thought about this. "You know what? You should see if you could come back with us the day after tomorrow, when the monks take us to Pelt so they can get their stuff back from the museum." She tensed her fingers on the stone railing, toggling them back and forth. Not looking at Drgnan Pghlik at all, just looking out into the night, Katie asked him, "Would you . . . um . . . You know, there's a dance at the school this weekend. I, you know, I kind of wanted to go with this one guy, but, um, it turns out he can't go? Because he . . ."

Drgnan waited, listening closely.

"Because he broke both his legs. Under a. Um. Dog. And so, maybe you could, you know. You could. Yeah. Go with me."

Drgnan Pghlik cast his eyes down shyly. "I would embarrass you," he said. "And you will want to be at the side of your friend with the broken legs."

"You wouldn't embarrass me," said Katie. "Not at all."

"I would," said Drgnan Pghlik. "I cannot do the dances of the other states. I can do only the dances of Delaware. And as I have said, when we monks dance, we levitate, so you and I would be spinning around in the air, whirling together off the ground, over the heads of everyone else."

"Flying?"

"You have seen me drift away from the ground."

"Flying dancing?"

"Yes."

Katie swallowed and turned toward him. "Yeah," she said, her eyes a little hungry. "That . . . the flying while dancing? That wouldn't be so much of a problem."

"What about your broken-legs friend? Do you not need to apply heat to his knees and feed him ices from a spoon?"

"I lied. There was just this guy I liked. I thought he was cool. But I was never going to go with him to the dance. He doesn't even know I exist."

Drgnan Pghlik mused, "But do you exist? Do I? Perhaps both of us are merely a passing dream in the mind of—"

Katie clapped her hand over his mouth. "You

know?" she said. "Sometimes a girl just wants a guy to be the silent, mysterious type."

Under her palm, she could feel him smiling.

I could tell you now how they left the gangsters, all tied up, down in a village where the authorities would find them, stacked like cordwood. I could tell you how the monastery was blotted out with fog and how if someone had sought it again, they wouldn't have been able to find it, for it was no longer where it had been.

I could whisk us several days into the future, and I could tell you how Jasper, Katie, Lily, and Drgnan Pghlik all set off in the gang's white van, along the broken, unused highway; I could tell you whether the trip was uneventful, with the monks driving, listening to techno, while the four kids sat in the back playing Travel Scrabble without vowels, or whether there were tremendous adventures yet to come before they made it home to Pelt. I could tell you whether or not Mr. Lecroix from the Pelt Museum was imprisoned for buying stolen artifacts, or how the school dance went, and whether Katie and Drgnan Pghlik actually did whirl above the room to everyone's amazement; and I could tell you whether Choate was impressed, and gaped up from below, and how happy Lily was for her friend, because Lily thought Drgnan was the nicest person she'd ever met, and one of the most beautiful boys she'd ever seen—in fact, standing by the fruit punch bowl, she found herself even wishing that—

But instead, I would like to go back and end this book with the monks of Vbngoom dancing in their courtyard, because I wish sometimes that I were among them, and if I write about it, it will be like I was there.

Up on the wall, the three kids watched the ceremonial dance—Drgnan having run down to take his place among his brethren. In rows and columns, robed men turned and stomped. They felt the impact of their heels on worn stone, and at every step, their bodies were lighter.

Lily, Jasper, and Katie saw the dazzling patterns

below them shift and shake. The ceremonial horns blew—a sound more resonant and strong than any Lily had ever heard—and the monks of Delaware stomped and stomped in praise, in thanks for the day, in thanks for the night, in thanks for each other, for their order, their brotherhood, their ways.

And is it not right, always and everywhere to give thanks? For D E L A W A R E has been given unto us, all of us—the realm of our hopes, the land of our dreams and distortions. Each of us hides our own private Delaware lost in the gray jungle-tangle of our brains. No one else can know its depths and its byways. No one else can know the height of its towers, the secrets of its tides and pools. There will always be lost lagoons to find there, and ruins almost hidden by the sand. There will always be monsters of great beauty and good men with ugly frowns. The forests are dark, but lights bob among the branches. You are at home there, more at home than anyplace else, and yet you will never go there in your life. Their legends are yours. The pirates sail around the cape, a crew of skeletons in the rigging. Milkmaids run down mountain passes, dragging kites behind them. Wizards crack their backs after long days of chalk and incantation while above the crowded bazaars, over the golden temples, against the setting sun, around the ruddy minarets, the pterodactyls call out a long farewell.

Lily raised her hands over her head, and felt, between her fingers, the night air, alive.

FAIR DELAWARE

Do you seek a summer moon?
Do you seek a warm lagoon?
Would you like a sun that sets
Over domes and minarets
In a land of monks and maidens fair?
Seek Delaware—
Delaware, Delaware.

Do you like a grand bazaar
And snacks made of bears and tar?
D'you seek wise men with strange powers?
And goats in hotel showers?
Forget Rhode Island. Who'd go there?
Try Delaware—
Delaware, Delaware.

From the burning brooks of New Castle
To the blowzy fields of Kent
To the pickle yards of Sussex,
That's where my youth was spent.
From the deserts of far Smyrna
To the griffon cotes of Zoar
To the maples of old Waples,
Oh, those happy days of yore!

Though I've seen New York and Rome
My heart longs for my old home.
I miss taxis pulled by yaks
And flying squirrel attacks

And barbarian lords with feathered hair,
In Delaware!
Delaware! Delaware!

[Fading:]

It's an East Coast state with a foreign flair.
Fair Delaware!
Where things are arched instead of square
In Delaware.
Young Jasper Dash learned how to stare
In Delaware.
Visit downtown Dover, if you dare,
State capitol of Delaware.
If you're eating candy, always share
In Delaware.
etc.

[Repeat until you have exhausted all possible rhymes and driven your parents crazy. Then fade, veiling your face and backing mysteriously—but quickly—out of the room.]

Fair Delaware

Words and Music
M. T. Anderson

de-serts of far *Smyr-na* to the grif-fon-cotes of *Zoar* to the

D.C. al Coda

map-les of Old *Wa*-ples, Oh, those hap-py days of *yo-re!*

Del-a-ware.

It's an East Coast state
Where things are arched
If you're eat-ing can -

repeat ad lib

with a foreign flair.
in — stead of square.
-dy, — al-ways share.

Fair *Del-a* — ware!
In *Del-a* — ware.
In *Del-a* — ware.*

*Visit downtown Dover, If you dare, State capitol of Delaware... etc.
[Until you have exhausted all possible rhymes and driven your parents crazy.
Then fade, veiling your face and backing mysteriously—but quickly—out of the room.]*

rall.

A LETTER FROM THE GOVERNOR OF DELAWARE

AUTHOR'S NOTE

Following the original publication of this book, it came to my attention that I had made a few errors in my depiction of the Blue Hen State. I don't know exactly what the problem was: Maybe the mountains actually extend farther to the east or maybe the dinosaur in the ruins really was a tyrannosaurus. Who knows? Anyway, some friends from Delaware accused me of having made major mistakes because I had "never been there" and had "made things up completely."

In my defense, I am including a letter from Delaware governor Jack Markell, who had the incredible generosity and good humor to write to me about the accuracy of this novel. I think the letter speaks for itself. For one thing, any state that has a governor who can write a letter like the following is a state worth celebrating.

Incidentally, this is the first time a state governor has called me buster.

STATE OF DELAWARE
OFFICE OF THE GOVERNOR
TATNALL BUILDING, SECOND FLOOR
WILLIAM PENN STREET, DOVER, DE 19901

JACK A. MARKELL
GOVERNOR

PHONE: ▓▓▓▓▓▓▓▓
FAX: ▓▓▓▓▓▓▓

September 14, 2009

M.T. Anderson
Award-Winning Author
Boston, Mass.

Dear Mr. Anderson,

After reading your book, *Jasper Dash and the Flame Pits of Delaware,* it is my sincere hope that you ~~never choose our state as a setting for a book ever again~~ enjoy tremendous success with this latest installment in your "Pals in Peril" series.

I am certain that the adventures of Jasper, Lily, Katie and Drgnan Pghlik will ~~lead to a great deal of geographical and cultural confusion among Delaware school children~~ serve as a valuable lesson in how to have fun with fiction!

Special thanks for including my mailing address on page 92 for those who wish to address inaccuracies in your representation of Delaware. We look forward to ~~shipping all of these letters straight back to you, buster~~ cheerfully answering each and every letter we receive from your curious and diligent readers.

I hope you will accept my sincere invitation (I'm being serious about this part) to visit our state again. My wife Carla and I would be delighted to have you as a guest for dinner at the Governor's Mansion. Please contact my scheduling secretary at ▓▓▓▓▓▓▓▓ if you are able to divert from your usual toll-booth-only tour of the First State to visit us in Dover. We'll set you straight on all things Delaware.

In the meantime, please accept this book about Delaware as a small token of our appreciation for bringing ~~embarrassment~~ attention to our fine state.

Sincerely,

Jack Markell

Jack Markell
Governor of Delaware

It is time we all talked about Delaware.

When I was a child, I loved books of fantasy travel and adventure: Victorians in pith helmets and starched collars knocking around in the dusty tombs of Karnak. Bookish mystery-seekers making their way across the frozen steppe to read the runes on some ancient, magical pillar dedicated to toads. Conan the Barbarian, smashing through lost jungles with spiders twitching above his head, flying apes perched in ruins to either side of him, cobras slithering to bite his knees, and a piranha in his canteen.

What thrilled me in these books were not just the specific moments of adventure—the fumbling mummies, the lassoed pterodactyls—but also the sense of the vast, untamed landscape. In my little, safe suburban house, I dreamed of a world of howling wilderness and secret valleys. I hoped that there were still places to discover on the Earth. And I hoped even more that there were still places that would remain undiscovered and unplundered until the end of time.

And so, as an adult, I have written a book about Delaware. Cut off from the world for generations by its prohibitive interstate tolls, Delaware, to most of us, is nothing but an exotic name, a realm of fantasy. I determined to pierce the veil of mystery. I determined to reach deep inside the Blue Hen State and yank out its giblets for all to see.

No, okay, I've never actually been to Delaware. I may not be one of your so-called "experts" on the state. But I have MapQuest, and any fool could tell you that Dragon Creek must be dragon infested, and Red Lion Creek must be red lion infested, and that Sandtown is a caravanserai in the middle of a desert. It doesn't take a PhD in geography to tell that seaside hamlets with names like Slaughter Beach and Broadkill Beach are the haunts of Vikings. You don't need to be a member of the Adventurers' Club to figure out that the largest building in Ogletown is an observatory, or to guess that when you visit the village of Bear, you better hide your food up a tree.

Jasper Dash and the Flame-Pits of Delaware is a homage to those adventure books I read as a kid, and to wonderful friendships, and to the imaginations of those of us who sit on lawn chairs and dream of far-off places. It is the story of three plucky kids who brave the interior of Delaware—who seek ancient artifacts—who confront dinosaurs and secret police—who are chased and marauded by Delaware's tyrannical leader, the Awful and Adorable Autarch of Dagsboro—but who, in the end, find their way home.

I hope you enjoyed reading it as much as I enjoyed writing it. And I hope that as you read it sitting at home, it took you places you've never been.

Like Wilmington.

**Turn the page for a sneak peek at
the next outrageous Pals in Peril Tale!**

VBNGOOM GONE

They came from the heights of the mountain, a long procession winding their way between the cracks and steeples of stone. The peak was hidden in fog. Through the ravines and over the hunched backs of granite the men padded, barefoot, all in a line, one after another, silent in the morning. They walked through the high, barren places where the ancient wind had licked the limestone into pillars and pits, caves and crevasses. There were two hundred boys and men, all dressed in flowing robes of green; and each one carried a small piece of a dismantled white van.

They marched through hollows carved by owling storms and mazes formed by no human

hand. The largest men carried the van's white doors, their heads sticking through the open windows, or they hefted a roof-panel between them. Others carried the exhaust pipe, the dashboard, the brake pads. The littlest boys—six or seven years old—carried single bolts cupped in their hands. The procession was led by two silent youths, frowning, walking side by side, both cradling the headlights in their arms. The line of them wandered through the bitter karst.

They were the monks of Vbngoom, called the Platter of Heaven, the most powerful monastery in the whole State of Delaware. They filed along dinosaur curves and great stone mounds.

Only three of the people in this solemn parade of broke-down van did not wear green robes and did not have their heads shaved.

Lily Gefelty, a slightly stocky girl whose bangs flapped down in her face or blew backward in a burst, depending on the wavering breeze, carried the crankshaft timing gear. Her eyes—when they appeared through her hair—

were bright, and she greeted each new vista with mute delight. She loved the mountain above them and the green forests down below. She loved that she was here with friends, and that they were on their way home after a satisfying adventure. She was very ready for home.

Behind her was Jasper Dash, Boy Technonaut. He wore a pith helmet and kept squinting into the haze, trying to make out the Delaware Canal or the smokestacks of far Wilmington. Unlike Lily, he was used to mountaintops, monks, and danger, having appeared in his own series of adventure books in which he pedaled blimps through the air, socked ruffians, and rode buffaloes bareback. Still, he also wanted to get home to his mother and his own bedroom and laboratory.

Katie Mulligan, behind him, wore the van's fan belt around her neck. She was used to adventure too, because she starred in a series called Horror Hollow, in which she unwound mummies, taught werewolves to heel, and

heavily salted leech invasions. Under other circumstances, she would have been grumpy about yet another adventure—she was getting tired of being bitten, stomped, and slimed—but on this particular day, she was in an extremely good mood, because right behind her walked Drgnan Pghlik, a young monk of Vbngoom who had agreed to go to the school dance with her.

It is unusual for monks to go to school dances—usually they spend their free time chanting in Latin, speaking in riddles, drawing cherubs in old books, and slapping themselves with stinging nettles—but Drgnan was a very unusual monk. For one thing, he was being trained as one of his monastery's Protectors and taught martial arts so that he could rove around the country, doing good and making sure that no pirate or plunderer threatened his sacred order and their secrets.

The monks climbed down the mountain. They were leaving their home. Or, to be more precise, their home was leaving them.

They all gathered to rest on a little plateau with pillars of limestone like a fallen palace of wax. Lily sat down and took out her water bottle. She unscrewed the lid and took a deep swig. She watched the monks carefully. She could tell something was going to happen, but she didn't know what.

She knew that it was time for a few of the monks to leave their home so that they could go out into the world—across the forbidden border of Delaware—to collect those sculptures and gold-bound manuscripts that had recently been stolen by gangsters. The monks would give Lily, Katie, and Jasper a ride home to Pelt, their town.

Hence the procession and the auto parts. The monks had dismantled the gangsters' white van. There was no road on this side of the mountain. They were carrying the van down the mountain to reassemble it near a road. Then Katie, Jasper, Lily, and Drgnan would drive with a few of the senior monks toward the border of Delaware. They would make their way

to Pelt and reclaim the artifacts illegally sold to the Pelt Museum.

But Lily didn't understand what the rest of the holy men were doing there, or why they seemed so sad.

One of the most revered of the monks, a forty-year-old man with a clever face and an uneven grin, came over to her and her friends. His name was Grzo, and he was in charge of the Scriptorium, the room where manuscripts were copied by the monks. Usually, he spent all his days there, in a hall silent but for the squeak of quill pens and the laser-y mouth-sounds of young monks drawing angelic wars.

Brother Grzo pointed up the slope, to where the monastery could still be seen through the thinning haze. He said to Drgnan, "Look up the mountain. There you see Vbngoom upon the top of Mount Tlmp for the last time."

Drgnan nodded. Lily, Jasper, and Katie looked confused and surprised. Brother Grzo explained, "Do not fear, children. You may someday see our home again, but not in this place. For two hundred years, Vbngoom has sat among the Four Peaks. It has moved among the mountains in the fog, shuffled like a pea among four nutshells to fool those who would seize upon our treasures and our sacred flames. But now that the gangsters of the World-Wide Lootery are in the hands of the govenment authorities, there is too much danger that we shall be found. Too many people know where our monastery is hidden. Too many roads lead to our mountaintop. Too many Delaware spies have asked too many questions. No longer can the monastery of Vbngoom hide in the clouds atop the Four Peaks. No longer is a jungle filled with kangaroo-riding cannibals and lisping serpent-men enough protection. Vbngoom must move farther away. Go and sit while we pray."

Katie, Lily, and Jasper crawled up into a small nook worn into the stone. Katie passed out sandwiches. They ate. They looked up at the

towers and walls of the place they had grown to love. They watched the monks form a great circle. Some stood on rough pedestals. Out of backpacks they drew pipes and rings that they fitted together to make horns and trumpets. A few trumpeters stood aloof on pillars, awaiting a signal.

An age was coming to an end.

The abbot of the monastery, an ancient man who walked on wooden crutches, began whispering a prayer. The others joined in, each in his own time. The plateau murmured, muttered. For a long time, this went on. An hour passed. The sun moved in the sky. The shadows on the monastery walls fell crooked, then straight. The pine trees around its base wriggled in the midday sun.

And all at once, the whispering stopped—the horns came up—a great, triumphant chord echoed through the mountains, blasting away at the mirage of what was.

In the silence that followed, Lily's ears rang. No monk spoke. The abbot shuffled out to the

middle of the ring of monks. He looked up at his home. He raised his palm and lay it beneath his lips. And he blew.

That tiny breath traveled up the mountainside—hit the pine trees like a gale—and the monastery began to unravel as if it was made of dry sand. Away flew a turret—and now walls were sifting off in clouds, blowing through the sky, brilliant, glittering—all of it—the trees on the peak, the volcanic crater, the cloisters, the bridges, the chapels, the banners—all of it swarmed through the air, locustlike, and tumbled off to the north.

Vbngoom migrated through the sky.

Lily cried at it shimmering in the noonday light.

Then there was no more monastery there— in fact, no more peak. Suddenly the monks were only a quarter mile from the top.

The kids were sad that Vbngoom could no longer stay atop Mount Tlmp, but glad it would be safe elsewhere.

Drgnan came to their side, wiping his eyes. The musicians were unscrewing their trumpets and dismantling their pipes and stowing them in backpacks. The rest said quick prayers and picked up their automotive parts.

Then the procession set off again, holding high their tappets, their clutch, their shocks.

Vbngoom was gone.

ABOUT THE AUTHOR

M. T. Anderson has not been seen for some years. Impersonators using his name on their books have won the *Los Angeles Times* Book Award, the *Boston Globe–Horn Book* Award, and the National Book Award. Mr. Anderson divides his time between an underground lair and (when he's on vacation) the inside of a public mailbox in Scranton.

Agents with classified messages, innocent citizens drawn haplessly into a web of terror, and dictators eager to deliver their insane demands for world domination can conveniently contact Mr. Anderson online via mt-anderson.com.